Telling Wilde Tales...

by Jules Tasca

Single copies of plays are sold for reading purposes only. The copying or duplicating of a play, or any part of play, by hand or by any other process, is an infringement of the copyright. Such infringement will be vigorously prosecuted.

Baker's Plays
7611 Sunset Blvd.
Los Angeles, CA 90042
bakersplays.com

NOTICE

This book is offered for sale at the price quoted only on the understanding that, if any additional copies of the whole or any part are necessary for its production, such additional copies will be purchased. The attention of all purchasers is directed to the following: this work is fully protected under the copyright laws of the United States of America, the British Commonwealth, including Canada, and all other countries of the Copyright Union. Violations of the Copyright Law are punishable by fine or imprisonment, or both. The copying or duplication of this work or any part of this work, by hand or by any process, is an infringement of the copyright and will be vigorously prosecuted.

This play may not be produced by amateurs or professionals for public or private performance without first submitting application for performing rights. Licensing fees are due on all performances whether for charity or gain, or whether admission is charged or not. Since performance of this play without the payment of the licensing fee renders anybody participating liable to severe penalties imposed by the law, anybody acting in this play should be sure, before doing so, that the licensing fee has been paid. Professional rights, reading rights, radio broadcasting, television and all mechanical rights, etc. are strictly reserved. Application for performing rights should be made directly to BAKER'S PLAYS.

No one shall commit or authorize any act or omission by which the copyright of, or the right to copyright, this play may be impaired. No one shall make any changes in this play for the purpose of production.

Publication of this play does not imply availability for performance. Both amateurs and professionals considering a production are strongly advised in their own interest to apply to Baker's Plays for written permission before starting rehearsals, advertising, or booking a theatre.

Whenever the play is produced, the author's name must be carried in all publicity, advertising and programs. Also, the following notice must appear on all printed programs, "Produced by special arrangement with Baker's Plays."

Licensing fees for TELLING WILDE TALES... are based on a per performance rate and payable one week in advance of the production.

Please consult the Baker's Plays website at www.bakersplays.com or our current print catalogue for up to date licensing fee information.

Copyright © 1986 by Jules Tasca
Made in U.S.A.
All rights reserved.

TELLING WILDE TALES...
ISBN **978-0-87440-618-4**
#49-B

CONTENTS

If all seven are done together, they can be played by a 4 males, 3 females ensemble, or, of course, different actors or actresses can play in each piece.

TELLING WILDE TALES

The Wilde tales take place on a bare stage. The sets are created by the actors from a group of multicolored wooden risers of different sizes. The actors' costumes consist of basic dark body suits, to which can be added capes, hats and masks to effect quick changes of character. The music can be flutes and drums to bridge the plays, but sound effects should be made by the players themselves whether they are visibly changing the risers around or passive to the action of the moment.

At opening the brightly colored risers are constructed into a short wall. SOUL enters into a spotlight and addresses the audience.

Soul. Good evening (afternoon) everyone. May I introduce myself briefly so we can get on with telling Wilde tales. I am a soul. A human soul. And I walk about like this because I'm cut off from my body, that of a fisherman. He was a victim of both love and the laws of the land and sea. But the fisherman's playlet comes a bit later. My personal interest always makes me jump to him. In fact, our first tale is about a birthday of a little girl. Not an ordinary little girl, oh, no, but the little daughter of a Spanish Monarch. The birthday of the Infanta.

The Birthday of the Infanta

The lights come up full as the other players rise up from behind the wall and form the risers into a throne room. Two males and two females begin playing "bullfight." One male has makeshift horns on his head and is charging the other male who has a napkin to use as a cape and a wooden sword in his belt. The Infanta, who wears frilly cuffs and collar, has a white flower in her hair. The other male character, the King, far upstage, looks over a tall riser. He wears a crown)

SOUL. *(To the audience)* I play the evil Don Pedro ... to the best of my ability, that is. For I have nothing in my background that fits me for the role. I am *(He puts on a plumed hat and black gloves)* the guardian of this little princess here. *(He strokes the Infanta's hair as she watches her birthday guests play in the royal ballroom. To the children)* Don't become too sweaty, children. The princess doesn't like to see sweat. *(DON PEDRO crosses up to the KING)* Your Majesty.

KING. What is it, Don Pedro?

DON PEDRO. Your Majesty, the Princess is downstairs. She waits for you to join her. The birthday party, remember?

KING. Of course, I remember. I can't. I just can't celebrate. This day that she was born ... This day that she was born, my Queen died.

DON PEDRO. Every year on her birthday you sink into dispair.

KING. I can't be joyous at a birth that cost so much. You've reared my daughter this long and this well. Stay with her. I cannot celebrate such a day. I cannot. I will have the priest say solemn Mass for my Queen.

DON PEDRO. *(As the KING exits)* But your Majesty, she asks for you ... She asks ... *(To audience)* He can't last much longer. The sentimental fool. And then I will be the force behind my protege, the next ruler of Spain. *(He crosses to the Infanta)*

INFANTA. Is he coming, Don Pedro?

DON PEDRO. I think not, Princess. He goes to pray for your mother. Again he turns your birthday celebration into a funeral Mass for her. Forgive him, poor Infanta. He means you no slight. It is a weakness.

INFANTA. Yes, Don Pedro, yes, it is. He'll spend the whole day in that gloomy chapel. You were right when you taught me that the weak should never have a throne.

DON PEDRO. Now, now, this is no day to fret. I will celebrate the cosmic event of your birth with you. Are you enjoying your little friends here?

INFANTA. You've taken me to see the real bull fights in Seville. These boys're just playing at it.

DON PEDRO. They're having fun.

INFANTA. *(To the playing children)* Kill the bull! Kill the bull! I want to see the bull killed! *(The other girls agree and cheer on the matador as he stabs the bull with his wooden sword and then stands with one foot on the fallen boy's back)*

DON PEDRO. Well done. Well done, boys. But now I have some real entertainment planned for the Princess. *(The four guests all gather around the INFANTA's throne keenly anticipating. DON PEDRO claps his hands)* First the tight rope walker. *(The children applaud, but not the Princess as a man in a clown's mask enters and mimes walking a tight rope)*

FEMALE GUEST. I've never seen a tight rope walker.

INFANTA. That's because you're not from a royal family. I have these tricksters come to the castle at my command.

MALE GUEST. You do? Anytime you want?

INFANTA. *(Yawning)* I've seen him so many times. The only time it's amusing at all is when he falls on his head.

DON PEDRO. *(As the rope walker goes off)* All right, the giant puppet then? *(The children all exude excitement. The INFANTA just folds her arms. DON PEDRO looking up)* So be it. The puppet. *(An actor with a pulcinella mask enters like a marionette on strings and prances around the children who scream with joy)*

FEMALE GUEST. It's so real!

INFANTA. The puppet master is up there on the balcony. See? We had him before.

DON PEDRO. The sweets in the puppet's hand are for you. *(The puppet gives each child a sweet. The INFANTA declines)*

INFANTA. *(Looking up)* Enough of this. *(The puppet bows and exits)* I don't want any candy to spoil my taste for that enormous birthday cake waiting for me in the dining hall.

MALE GUEST. How big is it, Princess?

INFANTA. It's as tall as I am. I don't even have to bend over to blow out the candles.

DON PEDRO. How about the snake charmer? *(He claps)*

FEMALE GUEST. *(As an old snake charmer enters with a basket)* My God, a real snake charmer?!

DON PEDRO. *(As Charmer begins playing flute over the basket)* Our sailors captured him on board a Moorish ship. He's a heathen, but we let him live because he has magic over the tempter of Eve. *(The snake pops his head out of the basket and begins rising. The children applaud and cheer)*

INFANTA. The snake is older than he is. It's not vicious at all. It doesn't even have a rattle. I don't like snakes anyway. Go away, old heathen. *(The Charmer covers the lid over the snake and exits)* I'm really not enjoying any of this, Don Pedro. I'm really not.

DON PEDRO. But you are too impatient, my Princess, for a special treat, something new.

INFANTA. Something I've never seen before? Promise? *(He nods)* What?

DON PEDRO. A monster.

INFANTA. *(As the others become fascinated too)* A real monster?

DON PEDRO. We just captured him yesterday. Two nobles hunting deer deep in the forest days from here where no civilized person goes saw him. Their sudden entrance scared the boy. But they tracked him down and bought him from his father who was glad to be rid of him.

INFANTA. Oh, where is he?!

DON PEDRO. Send the boy in, please. *(A boy with a distorted face who is slightly hunched enters smiling before the group. They all buzz to each other)*

INFANTA. *(Sotto)* Is that his real face from birth, Don Pedro?

DON PEDRO. *(Sotto)* I told you. A real monster, eh?

INFANTA. *(Sotto)* How could anything that ugly ... It's the devil himself. A perfect horror.

DON PEDRO. *(Sotto)* This is the part you're going to like, my Princess, he dances.

INFANTA. *(As others buzz louder)* He ... He can dance?

This ... This ... This can dance?

Don Pedro. Oh, yes. His name is Carlos.

Infanta. You there. Yes, you can come forward here. *(The boy crosses to the group)* Can you really dance, Carlos?

Carlos. I can dance. I dance to the songs of the wood cutters.

Infanta. He's not morose about being captured.

Don Pedro. No. And living in so remote a part of the country he's never seen a mirror. He doesn't even know he's grotesque. Bow to the Princess, Carlos.

Infanta. *(As CARLOS goes down on one knee)* So grotesque he's spellbinding. Oh, I want to see him dance. *(The children agree)* Up, up, I want you to dance. Don't call for the minstrels. We'll all make music ourselves. *(CARLOS rises. They all hum, rhythmically, clap, and bang the floor. CARLOS looks at them all and steps back)*

Don Pedro. Well, Boy, dance! Dance! This is the Princess of Spain and she wants you to dance for her. *(CARLOS smiles, basks in the attention of royalty. After a beat he begins to move his body with the music of the others. Then he breaks into a dance. The children love the dancing and increase the tempo of their music to make Carlos dance faster and faster. Even DON PEDRO joins in clapping until CARLOS dances so fast that he collapses. All applaud, the INFANTA the loudest)*

Infanta. He's the highlight of the day, Don Pedro!

Male Guest. Bravo, I say!

Female Guest. Yes, Bravo, Carlos!

Infanta. Come here, my wild dancer. *(CARLOS, out of breath, rises and crosses to the INFANTA. She takes the flower from her hair and gives it to him. He looks at the flower lovingly, after which, he presses it to his lips and sinks to one knee grinning with contentment. The others laugh at him)*

INFANTA. Don Pedro, I want him to dance again.

FEMALE GUEST. Oh, yes, yes, make him dance again.

DON PEDRO. He's spent just now, Princess. Why don't you go and cut that royal birthday cake. When you've all filled your stomachs, we'll have him dance again.

CARLOS. *(Putting the flower in his belt)* I would do it now. I would dance now. I would...

INFANTA. No, I do want the cake. We're all hungry. *(Sotto to DON PEDRO)* Don't let him come to the dining hall. We wouldn't be able to eat a thing with that face staring at us.

DON PEDRO. *(Sotto)* Of course, he'll always be kept in the basement unless you want him to perform. *(At the INFANTA's signal she and the other children run off merrily shouting. CARLOS starts after them)* No, Carlos, you wait here. When the Princess returns, you can dance for her again.

CARLOS. Yes, your Grace. I'll wait. Your Grace, what is cake?

DON PEDRO. Cake is a delicious concoction of eggs and flour and sugar. A birthday cake has the most wonderous decorations on top of it like the inside of a Cathedral, only done in all colored sugar and glazes and icings and...

CARLOS. I would love to go and see it.

DON PEDRO. Well you can't ... You ... You ... Well, I suppose it's time to stop all this whispering behind your back. Someone as ugly as you are, Carlos, would upset the...

CARLOS. Ugly? What is ugly?

DON PEDRO. It's a thing you are.

CARLOS. Really? I am? I am ugly?

DON PEDRO. Your father never told you that?

CARLOS. I never heard that word before, your Grace. Ugly. Ugly. It's such a pretty word, ugly. *(DON PEDRO laughs)* Maybe that's why the Princess gave me this flower because I'm ugly and she loves me.

DON PEDRO. Loves you? Come now, Carlos.

CARLOS. She didn't give this flower to any of the other boys.

DON PEDRO. You've never heard the word mocking either?

CARLOS. Mocking?

DON PEDRO. It's something that's done to the grotesque in the Spanish court here, Boy, for sport.

CARLOS. Grotesque?

DON PEDRO. Yes, as you are. Grotesque.

CARLOS. I'm proud to be grotesque, your Grace, for it has brought me to the palace and has made me a favorite of a beautiful princess.

DON PEDRO. Oh, you know the word beautiful, but you don't know ugly.

CARLOS. I know beautiful. It's what God puts into birds and flowers and animals to make us want to look at them a long time. Like a puppy's eyes or a white flower or ... or ... or the lips of a royal princess.

DON PEDRO. *(Laughs)* Why, I do believe by all that's sound that you've fallen in love with the Princess, the Infanta, herself! You!

CARLOS. Yes ... yes, your Grace. Yes, I have. I do love her.

DON PEDRO. And what, let us say ,if your dreams could come true and the Princess could be yours. What would it be like, you and she? The two opposite poles of life. A Princess and a ... and a ... what do you call yourself?

CARLOS. I am Carlos the son of the charcoal maker.

DON PEDRO. Yes, of course. The soot is still in your fingernails. Charcoal. The Princess' hands are like a dove's wing ... Carlos. Your first lesson here in the civilized world is that the children of kings are the children of kings and the children of charcoal makers are the children of charcoal makers. But in that warped fantasy you have I ask you to tell me. What would it be like, you and she, the beautiful one, together?

CARLOS. Be like? It would be like ... like ... Her and me would be playmates and ... and ... and ... I ... I would teach her all sorts of wonderous things.

DON PEDRO. Oh? What wonderous things?

CARLOS. I ... I ... I could ... I could teach her to make little cages out of weeds and rushes for the grasshoppers to sing in. And a flute. I can show her how to carve a flute out of a branch. *(He takes a wooden flute and plays a few notes)* That's the music hidden in the wood of trees.

DON PEDRO. The Infanta of this palace has a whole orchestra, a choir and innumerable minstrels to pleasure her ears. What else could you teach her?

CARLOS. What else? I ... Well ... I ... I know the cry of every bird and the trail of every animal and we, the both of us, could track a rabbit by its little foot marks in the ground. And, yes, I know where the wood pigeons bury their nests. Once I saw a fox snatch a wood-pigeon and you know what I did?

DON PEDRO. I can't imagine.

CARLOS. I brought the young ones home, nest and all, and raised them myself. They used to nip the food right out of my hand. Oh, the Princess would've like them, your Grace. And I have puppies at home, too and a big turtle. They're all so gentle and delicate. Oh, I know she'd love them.

DON PEDRO. Perhaps, the Princess does have a strong feeling for animals.

CARLOS. Then she would love the forest, your Grace. I do wish you'd let her go there some time. She could use my bed and I could sleep in the kitchen and we could...

DON PEDRO. Your day dream is becoming an impertinence.

CARLOS. I would teach her to dance like I do, your Grace. I know the autumn dance, the corn dance, the snow dance and best of all the dance of spring when the flowers come back. You know what I'm going to do for the Princess, your Grace? The first thing when we become better friends, I'm going to make her a necklace of red berries. I'm very good at making them. I take my time and they turn out real nice, and when she wears that necklace, I'll put fireflies in her hair so she'll look like one of God's saints, your Grace.

DON PEDRO. I've heard enough of this wishful thinking. It's no longer amusing to me. It's ... it's...

CARLOS. It's what, your Grace?

DON PEDRO. It is ugly. *(He claps his hands and two servants enter)* Have a mirror brought in here so that this forest dweller might for the first time see the truth. *(The two ser-*

vants arrange two thick risers horizontally and place one across the top vertically to create a full length mirror)

CARLOS. What is a mirror?

DON PEDRO. A glass that tells the truth. There are philosophers, Carlos, who tell us that there is nothing so beautiful as the truth.

CARLOS. Is that so? And I'm to be allowed to see this glass, your Grace? Can't I wait for the Princess to come back so we can see into the glass together?

DON PEDRO. The Princess has looked into a mirror thousands of times.

CARLOS. Thousands of times. I guess she would have the right to see the truth thousands of times. She's the Princess.

DON PEDRO. Yes, but now because you performed so well and pleased the Infanta and her friends, you are entitled to that joy. Go. Go, Carlos. It's all right to go to the mirror. *(CARLOS slowly crosses to the mirror)* It's perfectly all right to look in. Don't be afraid. *(As CARLOS looks into the mirror, another actor made up the same way as CARLOS plays the mirror image. CARLOS sees the image mimes the consternation of the deformed boy. CARLOS runs back to DON PEDRO. The servant snicker. DON PEDRO dismisses the servants with a wave of his hand and they exit)*

CARLOS. There was something ... There was something in that mirror.

DON PEDRO. Yes, that's the purpose of a mirror, my boy. Go again and look at that something. *(DON PEDRO gently shoves CARLOS back in the direction of the mirror and CARLOS slowly crosses up to the mirror again and again his "image" appears. This time CARLOS only takes a few frightened steps backward. He turns to DON PEDRO)*

DON PEDRO. You see. It cannot hurt you.

CARLOS. Cannot ... cannot hurt. *(He looks back at the mirror. He frowns; the image frowns. He slowly touches the mirror and his hand meets the hand of his image. He laughs; he holds his hands to his hips; he bows; he shouts; he puts his face up against the glass and the image conforms to his every gesticulation. CARLOS puts his hand to his mouth in fear and quickly crosses back to DON PEDRO)*

CARLOS. That boy ... that boy ... that ... that...

DON PEDRO. Yes, Carlos.

CARLOS. That boy ... that ... that ... I have never seen anything like that boy. His face ... that face ... that...

DON PEDRO. That boy is what is called ugly.

CARLOS. Ugly? That beautiful word ugly for such as the likes of him?

DON PEDRO. Ugly is the opposite, Carlos, of beautiful. The Princess is beautiful and that ... that in the mirror is...

CARLOS. Ugly. *(He crosses back to the mirror. His image reappears. He brushes the hair away from his eyes. The image follows suit)* You ... You are ... are ugly. Don Pedro, his Grace, says you are. Don Pedro? Everything that's in this room — the tapestry and the paintings and the furniture — everything's in ... in the mirror too ... with ... with the ... the ugly boy.

DON PEDRO. *(Laughs)* That's what a mirror does, Carlos. It shows you what lies before it.

CARLOS. What ... what ... whatever lies before it?

DON PEDRO. An exact copy of whatever is trapped in it reflection. What the echo is to the ear, the mirror is to the eye.

CARLOS. I even see another Don Pedro in there now. *(He takes the flower from his belt and raises it to his lips. He kisses it as his image copies his every move)* Then since I stand before it ... it is ... this is ... I am ... *(He points)* This out of shape boy is ... is ... They were laughing at this ... at me ... why ... why didn't my father kill me? Why? *(He tears the flower to pieces as does his image. Then he crosses down stage)* Take it out of here! Take the mirror away! Take that boy away. I beg you, your Grace! *(He falls down on the floor and DON PEDRO claps. the servant enter. DON PEDRO signals them to remove the mirror. CARLOS begins to sob as the INFANTA enters finishing a piece of birthday cake)*

INFANTA. His dancing was funny, but his acting is even funnier.

DON PEDRO. The cake was delicious?

INFANTA. Better than last year even. They're all out there feasting. I want him to dance for us again outside in the garden.

DON PEDRO. Then he will.

INFANTA. Get up. Get up and dance for us again. You're better than puppets and snake charmers. You must dance for me again.

DON PEDRO. Get up, Carlos.

INFANTA. I shall call him ugly Carlos. Ugly Carlos. *(She laughs)*

CARLOS. *(Up on his knees)* But ... but ... I ... I love you. Don't call...

INFANTA. Love me? *(She laughs)* You are as funny as the Barbary apes that Don Pedro had for my birthday last year and much more ridiculous. *(CARLOS bows his head)* Don Pedro, he's sulking. You must make him dance for me again or my whole birthday celebration will be ruined, absolutely ruined!

Don Pedro. He will dance for you again, sweet beautiful Princess. Carlos, get up and stop pouting. You must dance. The Princess commands you. Carlos! *(CARLOS doesn't move. The INFANTA folds her arms and taps her foot at Don Pedro. DON PEDRO removes his gloves and slaps CARLOS)* You ugly little monster! You animal from the wild! You must get up and go out to the garden and dance! The Infanta of Spain wishes to be amused! *(CARLOS still doesn't move)*

Infanta. A whipping is what the foul ugly looking thing needs! Ugly Carlos needs a whipping. *(CARLOS sobs one last final outburst of despair and slumps over at their feet. DON PEDRO kneels and feels his chest)* Send for the whipping master, Don Pedro; that'll make him dance.

Don Pedro. My majestic Princess, your funny little monster will never dance again. It's a pity. One as ugly could've perhaps made even your father smile.

Infanta. But why will he never dance again? I'll take the whip myself. I'll give him fifty...

Don Pedro. He would not even feel one. He's dead.

Infanta. Dead?! On my birthday? Why? Why is he dead, Don Pedro?

Don Pedro. Because his heart is broken, young beauty.

Infanta. Hmm. So. I'm issuing an order.

Don Pedro. An order, Princess?

Infanta. Yes. I won't have any other day ruined like this one. In future, Don Pedro, let those who come to entertain me have no hearts. I'm going for another piece of cake. And Don Pedro, I really am very very disappointed.

DON PEDRO. *(As the INFANTA exits)* Yes, dear one, I can understand that ... anyone could.
(The lights fade as SOUL steps out into a spotlight and addresses the audience)

SOUL. Oh, that horrible Don Pedro. I'm glad I'm not to be him anymore. It's a good thing, I'm told, there aren't too many of his kind in the world. As for the Infanta, as much as we'd all like to thrash her, we really can't blame her too much. I mean, after all, she has been brought up to be a Princess. As a respite in the next tale, The Star Child, I play nothing evil. *(He is handed an ax, a baby wrapped in a blanket, and a woolen hat which he puts on)*

THE STAR CHILD

WOODCUTTER. I am, among other people, the goodly woodcutter that you see now arriving home from the woods. *(The WOODCUTTER crosses back upstage where the risers have been formed into a fireplace, table, and stools. The WOODCUTTER's wife in apron and cap patomimes stirring a large pot)*

WIFE. Back so soon? Where's the firewood?

WOODCUTTER. There's enough to last until morning. Listen to what I've seen tonight.

WIFE. *(Taking the baby)* Where'd you get this child?

WOODCUTTER. Have you ever seen a more beautiful baby?

WIFE. Are you watching over it for someone?

WOODCUTTER. No. No, I'm not. I was out in the forest and I was about to start chopping away when in the distance a bright light, a star in the sky slipped down the wall of night and seemed to land behind a clump of willow trees.

WIFE. By God, husband!

WOODCUTTER. I thought for sure there'd be a pot of gold for whoever got to that spot. I ran to the willows so hard I scratched my face on the branches in the thicket. And lo and behold when I got there to the point where the star fell...

WIFE. How much gold was there, Husband? Tell me!

WOODCUTTER. There was no gold, Wife. None. No treasure but this babe wrapped in the cloak and with this little amulet around his neck.

WIFE. And you brought him home here?

WOODCUTTER. 'Twould be evil to leave a child to the deadly knife of a winter frost.

WIFE. But ... but does this mean, Husband, that we must keep him?

WOODCUTTER. Goodly wife...

WIFE. Look in this pot. We hardly have enough to feed our own babes that sleep in the next room. And who knows it might bring us bad fortune, this orphan.

WOODCUTTER. It wouldn't, my wife. It's a star child.

WIFE. It's another mouth to feed, another child to

dress, another ... *(The other actors make the sound of winter wind)* What is that?

WOODCUTTER. The door has blown ajar.

WIFE. It's a bitter chill. Close it tightly.

WOODCUTTER. *(Pantomiming closing the door)* In a house where a heart is hard a shut door will not keep out the chill. *(The WOODCUTTER's wife drops her head. He touches her face. She looks up into his eyes)*

WIFE. You are right. It's just that sometimes it is so hard to do what is right. I shall put this child in with our youngest. *(The sound of the wind now stops. The WOODCUT-TER kisses his wife and then the baby. The WOODCUTTER crosses down to the audience)*

WOODCUTTER. The star child grew up to be the most handsome boy anyone had ever seen. But this beauty was a deadly worm that ate up all in him that was good. *(As the WOODCUTTER goes off, the STAR-CHILD, wearing a radiant smiling mask, runs on with two other boys and a girl. They sit at the table and clamor for breakfast)*

STAR-CHILD. I'm waiting! I'm waiting! I like to have my breakfast on time, Stepmother!

WIFE. *(Entering with wooden bowls and spoons)* All right! Patience!

BOY 1. Mother, you know the Star-Child has no patience.

GIRL. Yes, Mother.

WIFE. His name isn't Star-Child. It's...

STAR-CHILD. I won't use any name you gave me, Step-mother. I'm not your son.

WIFE. *(Exiting)* Maybe it's a good thing you've never let me forget it, Lad.

STAR-CHILD. Last one to finish his barley meal is a village idiot. (*They all race to finish their meal. The STAR-CHILD finishes first, turns his bowl over and laughs at the others. He rises*)

BOY 2. He's won again.

GIRL. He always wins.

STAR-CHILD. You all like to compete with me. Then you grouse when you lose. The Star-Child has something extra to him. Let's go out into the woods. (*The four cross to another part of the stage. The others make the sounds of crows and owls and other forest creatures as they stand a few long risers up to be trees*)

GIRL. Let's rest by this oak tree. I'm so out of breath.

BOY 1. Me too.

STAR-CHILD. I'm not tired at all. I don't know why I even play with you three or any of the others down in the village. You're all sons and daughters of peasants.

BOY 2. But you don't even know who your parents are, Star-Child.

STAR-CHILD. I know this. I know in my heart that destiny has made me a Star-Child, born on a burst of light through the heavens. Your father told me it was so. I know I'm no mere peasant the way you all are.

BOY 1. What I want to know is what're we going to do today?

STAR-CHILD. (*As a blind man slowly enters*) I'll tell you what. Load up your hands with stones and let's drive this blind man from our woods.

GIRL. But he's only an old blind man.

BOY 2. We shouldn't, Star-Child.

STAR-CHILD. You'll all do as I say or I won't play with you any more, any of you. Do you hear me? *(The four pantomime picking up stones. The STAR-CHILD mimes throwing the first one and the blind man holds his head)* A hit! Let's see one of you match that ... Throw! ... Throw, I say! ... Whoever doesn't hit him is a peasant! A worthless peasant! Aim for his head! I hit the first try! Throw! *(The other children pantomime throwing stones. The blind man holds his face and chest. Then he runs off in pain. The STAR-CHILD laughs)* Run! Run, old man! Report us to the authorities! Give them a full description! *(He laughs again)* You all missed his head. *(To the Girl)* And you missed completely.

GIRL. I missed purposely, Star-Child.

STAR-CHILD. Then you are more a peasant than your brothers. I order you to go home ... Well. Go home! *(The GIRL begins to cry and runs off. To the Boys)* Come on you two. Let's see who can kill the most rabbits and squirrels today. Come on, sharpen some sticks. Do come on. *(As the BOYS exit, the others sing a Gregorian Chant sotto and lean two risers together to form a gothic arch. A cross on top of the arch completes the church. A priest enters reading his breviary. STAR-CHILD calls from off)* Father?

PRIEST. I'm up here, young man. *(The STAR CHILD enters through the arch and crosses to the priest)* So, you've finally gotten here. An hour late.

STAR-CHILD. I didn't want to come in the first place.

PRIEST. Where were you? Casting stones at the blind? Teasing beggars? Torturing God's animals?

STAR-CHILD. I get enough lecturing from the Wood-cutter.

PRIEST. That has no effect on you. You don't listen.

STAR-CHILD. He's not my father. I am sprung from a star. You know that.

PRIEST. I can see why he asked me to do something with you. When you look in this mirror, young one, *(He holds up a hand mirror)* what in God's name do you see?

STAR-CHILD. What do I see?

PRIEST. Look deep. What do you see. Be truthful.

STAR-CHILD. I see a handsome boy. A Star-Child. One whom all admire, Father.

PRIEST. Isn't that vanity? And is not vanity...

STAR-CHILD. I won't listen to silly proverbs. Some have a special destiny and it shows even in their outward appearance, Father. You said to be truthful. It pleases me to look at myself. It's not vanity to tell the truth.

PRIEST. And what is the destiny that's made manifest in your face?

STAR-CHILD. I'm waiting for it to be revealed to me.

PRIEST. But while you're waiting for this special call from destiny, why do you hate living things so much that you harm them?

STAR-CHILD. I ... Me? Me, Father?

PRIEST. The whole village knows, young man, that you badger the weak for sport, you maim birds and blind animals and destroy...

STAR-CHILD. It passes the time while I wait for my special destiny. The animals are dumb beasts and the weak are ... are ... well, they're just in the way sometimes. Worthless and in the way.

PRIEST. *In the way?!* How — how can anyone have the patience to counsel one such as you?! What you are doing is sinful! Do you think a man of sin will ever have a special destiny

STAR-CHILD. Sin? Father, there are many in the world who say that your theology's outmoded, that there is no sin. There is only us: the strong and ... and the weak. *(He hands the mirror back to the PRIEST)*

PRIEST. And that's what you believe?

STAR-CHILD. It's not belief. It's simply, Father, what the world is. The stong see the truth, that's all. Good day, Father. *(The STAR-CHILD exits. The PRIEST removes his cossack and puts on the woodcutter's hat. The WOODCUTTER addresses the audience as the others set up the fireplace, table and stools of the WOODCUTTER's home)*

WOODCUTTER. The boy was right. He did have a special destiny, different from anyone in the kingdom. And one day, not long after this meeting with the priest, the Star-Child's destiny came hobbling into my humble home. *(A raggedly dressed beggar woman crosses to the WOODCUT-TER)*

BEGGAR WOMAN. Are you the woodcutter, Sir?

WOODCUTTER. Yes, I am. I can spare you some soup and bread if you...

BEGGAR WOMAN. I've not come to beg today, Sir. I've come to chide you. What kind of man would bring up a son who'd stone an old beggar woman peacefully beggin' for a few pennies?

WOODCUTTER. My son?

BEGGAR WOMAN. They said it's the woodcutter's boy. He made the others throw stones too. My back is all bruised.

WOODCUTTER. *(Calling off)* Children, get in here! *(The STAR-CHILD along with the WOODCUTTER's two sons and his daughter enter)*

BEGGAR WOMAN. Sure, these are the ones, and he's the leader.

WOODCUTTER. I don't have to ask if what she says is true. I know it is. You've hurt so many people.

STAR-CHILD. Whatever she said is a lie. She's a foul beggar woman. You'd take her word over mine?

WOODCUTTER. Know you no mercy? Why is your heart unfeeling? What has this poor unfortunate done to you?

STAR-CHILD. Who are you to question me?

WOODCUTTER. My wife and I reared you and...

STAR-CHILD. Regardless, you're not my father. I'm not your son to cringe at your scowling face.

WOODCUTTER. Never did you speak truer! Yet remember I had pity on you when I found you in that cold forest out there the night the star came down to earth. *(The BEGGAR WOMAN, hearing this, swoons; the other children catch her and take her to sit down)* Get your mother, Girl. *(The GIRL exits)* What is it, Old Woman?

STAR-CHILD. Don't tell me you're going to bed and board her just because she fainted.

WOODCUTTER. *(As WIFE and DAUGHTER enter)* Be quiet!

WIFE. What is this? Who is she?

BEGGAR WOMAN. You say you found this child that night the star fell?

WOODCUTTER. Yes, old friend.

BEGGAR WOMAN. After years of searching...

STAR-CHILD. What is this babble?

BEGGAR WOMAN. Please, Sir, Madame, what did you find with him?

WIFE. Why ... a little chain about his neck.

BEGGAR WOMAN. With an amber amulet.

WOODCUTTER. It was. But how did you...

BEGGAR WOMAN. And a cloak of gold cloth with blue stars around the border.

WIFE. Exactly. I'll get them.

STAR-CHILD. *(As WIFE exits)* This demented old woman is trying to gain some advantage over us.

WOODCUTTER. Do you know something of this Star-Child, old one?

STAR-CHILD. I would throw her out and beat her for her arrogance. Instead, you treat her as though there was some truth to her ploy to steal something from us.

WIFE. *(Entering with amulet and cloak)* These are the child's only possessions.

BEGGAR WOMAN. *(Taking them)* Oh, yes! Dear God, yes! *(She cries)*

GIRL. What is it, Mother?

WIFE. I don't know.

BEGGAR WOMAN. He ... He ... Oh, God ... He is my son.

STAR-CHILD. Tell her to go! ... Well? Tell this lying old beggar to go! I won't eat any lunch or supper and I'll stay out all night if she stays here another minute!

BEGGAR WOMAN. He ... He is my little son. I lost him in the forest that night. *(STAR-CHILD laughs and gets the other children to laugh)*

WOODCUTTER. Stop! Stop it, I say! Let this woman speak!

BEGGAR WOMAN. I prayed to God. I searched the whole world looking for him.

STAR-CHILD. Everyone knows I'm not your son. She could've easily heard about me. A beggar picks up more than coins and they're wily in their way. She's here to cheat us out of something.

BEGGAR WOMAN. I am your mother.

STAR-CHILD. You're a mad woman!

WIFE. No one knew of this cloak and amber charm. No one. Not even my own children. I kept them at the bottom of my trunk. Only she who lost you would...

STAR-CHILD. You're as mad as she is! She's an ugly old beggar in rags. She couldn't be my mother! Look at her face!

BEGGAR WOMAN. *(Rising)* But you are my son. I carried you through the snow that night when robbers accosted me. I hid you under a tree and ran so they wouldn't steal you away from me. Since that night I've searched for you. Is it too late to share a mother's love?

STAR-CHILD. If you really were my mother, it would've been better if you'd stayed away from me forever.

BEGGAR WOMAN. But why?

STAR-CHILD. Because ... because ... because you have ... You have brought me shame. I thought I was born on the light of a star and now you — look at you — you come here and tell me that I'm a beggar's boy.

BEGGAR WOMAN. Don't speak to me so. Let me hold you and kiss you.

STAR-CHILD. You kiss me? You're mad. Go from here, whoever you are, and never let me see you again.

BEGGAR WOMAN. But I've suffered so much to find you.

STAR-CHILD. I would rather hold and kiss a bull frog!

Go! *(The BEGGAR WOMAN exits crying. The STAR-CHILD crosses to the other children)* Come on. Let's go check our rabbit traps. *(The children follow him off)*

WIFE. That boy should've been left to freeze those many years ago.

WOODCUTTER. He makes us all angry but don't say that. I have a few coins here. I'll run after the old beggar and give them to her. I do believe she is this boy's mother and we must ... *(Off we hear a long lingering tormented cry. The WOODCUTTER's three children run on frightened and cross to their parents)*

BOY 1. Mother! Father!

WOODCUTTER. What is it?

GIRL. Something happened to...

BOY 2. It's the Star-Child!

WIFE. What happened? Is he hurt? *(Slowly the STAR-CHILD enters from up center. The mask he now wears shows a deformed face. The others back away in fear)*

STAR-CHILD. I saw my reflection in the well! I stopped to drink and I saw ... I saw...

GIRL. Oh, please, don't come near me! You're as foul as a toad!

BOY 2. Star-Child, I can't believe it's you.

WIFE. What is this, my Husband?

WOODCUTTER. I don't know. It doesn't even look like him.

STAR-CHILD. But it is ... I am ... the Star-Child.

WOODCUTTER. This has come about surely because of you accursed ways, Child.

STAR-CHILD. The worst of which is denying my own mother. What shall I do? Someone tell me, please.

WIFE. You must go find your mother. You must travel through the whole world. You mustn't rest until you've found her.

STAR-CHILD. Yes. Oh, yes I must … I must find her and beg forgiveness. I have seen more in the well water reflection than this hideous face. It is more than the face of a brute. It is my heart shown to the world. I ask forgiveness of you all and I say goodbye. *(The STAR-CHILD runs off as the WOODCUTTER crosses down to address the audience. The lights dim behind him as the others making the animal sounds of the forest set up the risers to represent the woodland scene)*

WOODCUTTER. The Star-Child ran away deeper into the forest than anyone had ever been. Day and night he cried out...

STAR-CHILD. *(Appearing from behind tree as lights come up full and the WOODCUTTER goes off)* Mother! Mother! Mother come back! Let me see you once more, Mother! *(He begins to cry. After a beat, one of the actors with a blanket over him enters as a mole)* You! You there! Mole! Stop!

MOLE. I can tell by your voice you're the Star-Child. What is it? What could you want of me?

STAR-CHILD. A mole can see deep inside the earth. Tell me, is my mother hiding there someplace?

MOLE. You have blinded my eyes, remember. I see nothing now. I only hear the sorrow of the world.

STAR-CHILD. *(As the mole exits)* Mother! It is I! Mother, please, come back! Won't you? *(Another actor enters as a linnet with his arms inside a pullover)* You! You bird! Linnet, come here!

LINNET. So, it's true. The Star-Child has become a beast.

STAR-CHILD. Never mind. You can fly over all of us. Fly the whole earth and find my mother.

LINNET. You mock me. I can't fly. It was you who clipped my wings, Star-Child. It was you who did this. *(He exits as another actor races on and darts around the Star-Child)*

STAR-CHILD. Squirrel! Stop squirrel! *(The SQUIRREL stops)* Squirrel, you know this whole wood. Please tell me where I might find my mother.

SQUIRREL. You killed mine, Star-Child. Are you looking to kill yours too? Huh? No mother is safe with you. *(The SQUIRREL runs off)*

STAR-CHILD. Wait! Wait! Come back! *(Softly crying, the STAR-CHILD slowly exits as the WOODCUTTER steps on and watches him go)*

WOODCUTTER. *(To the audience)* For three years the Star-Child walked the whole world, a world where he found no caring or consideration for himself. His face and form moved no heart to charity. *(He steps off as the STAR-CHILD runs on. He is followed by children who stone him until he runs off)*

BOY 1. Get out!

BOY 2. Get out of our village!

GIRL 1. How he stinks!

GIRL 2. And how ugly he is! Frog face!

ALL FOUR. Frog face! Frog face! Frog face! *(Etc. They chase the STAR-CHILD off. Then he enters from another part of the stage. He is walking now. He approaches one of the risers and knocks. A farmer appears from behind the riser)*

FARMER. By the Lord God, what are you?

STAR-CHILD. Look, Farmer, I'm a young man. I'm about the world seeking the mother I've lost. I need a place to sleep tonight and some food. Just some bread would do, thank you.

FARMER. I have no spare room. And before you ask if you can sleep in the barn. No. That skin of yours'll mildew the corn. I won't waste bread on one so bestial. Your kind should just be left to the hand of God. Now go on your way before my wife comes out. She has a weak stomach for freakish things. *(The farmer disappears behind the riser)*

STAR-CHILD. But I'm not a freak! I'm one of God's creatures! I am one of God's ... I am ... And I need ... I need ... By God, answer me up there, where does a man go when there is no one? Answer me! Answer me!
(He listens for a beat. The other actors off make the animal sounds of the woods. Slowly, the STAR-CHILD exits. The WOODCUT-TER steps back on stage as the others make an archway from three of the risers. A soldier in helmet and carrying a spear, stands guard before the arch)

WOODCUTTER. One night the Star-Child emerged from the steaming summer forest and came to the gate of an immense walled city. The guard at the gate upon seeing the Star-Child approach shouted...

GUARD. *(As STAR-CHILD enters)* Halt! What is it you want in our fair city?

STAR-CHILD. I seek my mother here.

GUARD. Who is your mother?

STAR-CHILD. She's a beggar. I pray only to find her.

GUARD. Your mother would be better off not seeing what you've become. Leave our city gate. Go back to the marshes and pray that the earth will swallow you up. *(As the STAR-CHILD turns to exit, a man dressed as a wizard pops up from behind a riser)*

WIZARD. You there! Stop, Lad! *(STAR-CHILD stops)* What've we got here?

GUARD. A beggar, Sir. A foul beggar son of a beggar. I'm driving him away.

WIZARD. May I buy him from you?

STAR-CHILD. Buy me?

GUARD. Him? He's worth nothing. Who'd want him?

WIZARD. *(Offering the guard a coin)* The price of a goblet of sweet wine just to seal it ... I insist. Take, take, take it. *(The GUARD takes the coin)*

GUARD. Thank you, Sir. He's yours. Take him.

STAR-CHILD. *(As Guard exits inside the arch)* What ... What do you want with me?

WIZARD. You only need know that you are mine, that you are a slave of a great wizard.

STAR-CHILD. You're the first person in years to want anything of me. Why?

WIZARD. I'm an alchemist, a wizard, a magician. I've studied the black arts up and down the Middle East. I know. I know what I need. You see, Foul-Faced Monster, there are three pieces of the purest gold in the forest behind this city. According to the magic of this forest, only a bought slave can find them. Today when the sun comes up you will go out into those woods and fetch the gold for me. If you fail, I'll have your life.

STAR-CHILD. And what's to stop me from just going on my way?

WIZARD. You've wandered into a strange land, Beast-Child. According to the magic of this forest, if an honestly bought slave does not return to his owners, that slave dies at day's end. So, be on your way now. The only way you can live is to return to me with the gold. *(The WIZARD pushes the STAR-CHILD off stage. Then he exits, as the others make the sounds of the woods and turn the city gate into trees. The STAR-CHILD enters and hears crying)*

STAR-CHILD. Who's there? Who's there? Answer me! *(From behind a tree peeks an actor in white pullover who plays the rabbit)* Come out! Why, it's only a rabbit. Come all the way out.

RABBIT. I can't. *(The RABBIT show the STAR-CHILD that he's caught in a trap)* It's a hunter's snare. He'll be by here for it and me soon. I thought you were him. But he's probably a friend of yours and I'm as good as gone.

STAR-CHILD. I'm not a friend of his. But I know this kind of work well. *(He removes the leg trap from the rabbit)*

RABBIT. You're freeing me?

STAR-CHILD. Yes.

RABBIT. You must be a lover of God's creatures then.

STAR-CHILD. No, I don't think so. I don't know why I freed you. I'm a slave now myself and I guess I know the value of freedom.

RABBIT. Well, I thought I was dead. What can I do for you in return?

STAR-CHILD. There's nothing you can do. I'm the one who's dead. I'm obliged to find three pieces of gold for my master or pay with my life. In this endless forest I'll never find them.

RABBIT. But I know exactly where they are.

STAR-CHILD. You do?

RABBIT. Oh, yes. The white gold pieces that you seek are in a hole in the great fir tree over there. *(The RABBIT crosses with the STAR-CHILD over to one of the other risers)* Put your hand inside and simply take them. *(The STAR-CHILD reaches behind the riser and picks up the three gold pieces)*

STAR-CHILD. It's just as my master said. But why did you never take them?

RABBIT. The creatures of the forest are too clever to have any use for gold. It's too heavy to carry and can't be eaten. And no animal would make another a slave to get some.

STAR-CHILD. I never knew the creatures of the forest knew anything.

RABBIT. We know all we need to know.

STAR-CHILD. Well, we've saved each other's lives and that's all that matters now.

RABBIT. Yes, I gave to you as you gave to me. Goodbye now. I have thirty-one children at home and they're waiting for me. I will never forget you and neither will they.

STAR-CHILD. Thank you. Oh, God, thank you. With this gold I'll be able to go on my way and find my mother. *(He waves as the RABBIT runs off)* Farewell. I must get back before dark. I must ... *(A beggar with a bowl enters. He has a hood over his fae with only eye holes. Around his neck is a bell which rings as he crosses to the STAR-CHILD)*

BEGGAR. Alms. Anything you can spare. Alms, Sir?

STAR-CHILD. Who are you and why are you covered up?

BEGGAR. My face is covered because I am a leper, Sir.

My face is like a rotting apple.

STAR-CHILD. My face is such because I am a sinner. Let me pass and be about my business.

LEPER. Can you spare nothing? I must have money for the whole group of us. The wizard there has had us all thrown out of the city. We need money to travel to a new place where we can live what's left of our lives in peace.

STAR-CHILD. I have only what belongs to that wizard. I'm his slave. If I gave you what I have I'd...

LEPER. You'd what?

STAR-CHILD. *(Laughs)* It doesn't matter. *(He puts the gold pieces in the beggar's bowl)* Take this gold. Live the best you can. Your burden is more than mine. Your burden is for others. I'll die alone.

LEPER. This will save us all. This will truly save us all.

(As the lights dim, the LEPER exits and the STAR-CHILD goes off up stage. The WOODCUTTER steps out into a spot as the others set up the city gate and the guard takes up his position. When the STAR-CHILD enters this time, he has no mask on at all)

WOODCUTTER. The Star-Child headed back toward the city to wait for sun down and his doom. But this time as he passed through the gate of the city the guard bowed to him and cried out.

GUARD. How striking is the Lord! How exceptional! *(Others enter. WOODCUTTER becomes a priest)*

1ST MALE. Is this him?

PRIEST. Yes, it is.

1ST FEMALE. How handsome!

2ND FEMALE. He's more than handsome. He's beautiful!

GUARD. Surely, there is none to compare to him!

STAR-CHILD. Why are you all mocking me? Why?

2ND FEMALE. Why would anyone mock such a wonder as you, My Lord?

STAR-CHILD. How can you say I'm beautiful or handsome when my face is the picture of evil itself?

PRIEST. Look at your reflection in this woman's glass. Show him. *(2nd Female holds up her mirror to him)*

1ST FEMALE. Would you deny your own beauty?

PRIEST. It's a prophecy of this city that on this day one would come who would rule over us.

GUARD. I've waited all day.

PRIEST. As High Priest of this city I declare this man that one.

2ND FEMALE. Get him a scepter!

1ST MALE. We must crown him King! *(All ad lib agreement as the PRIEST holds out crown and scepter)*

STAR-CHILD. Stop this! I'm not worthy to be your king. I denied my mother and nothing can be right with me until she has forgiven me. Besides, my life is almost over today. Save your crown for a real king. *(He tries to exit. But coming through the city gate is the BEGGAR WOMAN, his mother, and the LEPER. The STAR-CHILD stops)* It's ... It's my mother. She ... She...

LEPER. Your mother is one of us.

STAR-CHILD. A leper too? *(The STAR-CHILD kneels down and kisses the feet of this mother and cries)* I denied you in pride. I ask forgiveness in humility, Mother, my mother. I gave you hate. But forgive me now and give me your love. Say you forgive me ... say it ... say it ... Speak to me. I have so little time. *(Pause. The Mother is silent)* Mother?

Mother, I want nothing, just your forgiveness. Then I'll wait for the sunset and my death ... Mother ... *(The BEGGAR WOMAN puts her hand on his head. She then removes her ragged cloak as does the leper. The man and woman are wearing crowns)*

MOTHER. Get up, Son.

STAR-CHILD. *(Rising)* Who ... What...

GUARD. It's the King and Queen! *(All bow and curtsy)*

MOTHER. *(Pointing to the King)* This is your father. To him you would have given your own life today.

FATHER. This, your mother, is my Queen. *(They all embrace the STAR-CHILD)* The Wizard is dead. I killed him myself so his evil no longer hold your life.

STAR-CHILD. But why, Dear Parents, did I have to go through all of this before I ... I ... I...

MOTHER. Suffering is the stuff of Star Children. That's why, Son. Now place the crown upon my son's head. *(The PRIEST crowns the STAR-CHILD and hands him the scepter)*

ALL. *(As PRIEST become the WOODCUTTER again)* Long live the young king! Long live the young king! Long live the young king! *(All freeze)*

WOODCUTTER. The young king had planned to rule wisely and justly. He planned to send me and my wife and children, indeed our whole village, many gifts and offerings of amendment for his past wicked ways. But he had suffered so much so long to right his wrongs and get to where he should have been in life that he died within a week of his coronation. *(The lights slowly fade on the tableau. In the dim light the others turn the risers into a town square. One of the actors puts on a gold covered doublet and cap, and holds a *sword. He stands on a riser in the center of the town square and assumes the position of a statue)*

THE HAPPY PRINCE

LITTLE GIRL. *(To her Mother)* I want a white lace parasol, Mother. Please, buy me one.

MOTHER. Stop whining, will you? We can't afford it. Why can't you be like the happy prince up there? He never cries for anything.

LITTLE GIRL. *(As they exit)* He's got a head of brass and a heart of lead He doesn't need a parasol to keep away the sun. *(A WOMAN passes with SOUL who wears a mortarboard hat and a monacle)*

WOMAN. He looks just like an angel, Professor.

PROFESSOR. How would you know? You've never seen an angel.

WOMAN. I have in my dreams, Professor.

PROFESSOR. Well just you stop all this dreaming. When a student of mine goes to bed, it should be for sleeping, nothing else. Dreaming is immoral. Go home and make soup or something. *(The PROFESSOR and his student exit as two men in top hats, the MAYOR and the TOWN COU-NSELOR enter)*

TOWN COUNSELOR. Mr. Mayor, in light of the poor harvest, what are people going to do?

MAYOR. There's food enough for us stored away. We'll just have to hope the people make it through somehow.

We can't worry about everyone.

SOUL. *(Enters as the MAYOR and TOWN COUNSELOR exit)* This is the statue of the happy prince. He's called by that name because, when he was alive and had a human heart, he didn't know what tears were. He lived in a palace of wide halls where sorrow was by edict forbidden to come near him. Now that he is dead and they've made him into a statue high on his pedestal at the town square here, he can see all the hardships in the city where he ruled. And even though his heart is made of lead, the misery he see makes him weep. *(As an actress with a commedia del arte half-mask of a bird enters and curls up under the statue, SOUL puts back on his mortarboard hat and crosses back up to the bird)*

PROFESSOR. Hm. Hm. Very odd. Extremely odd. Hm. A swallow. I've been a Professor of ornithology for thirty years and I've never seen a swallow this far north at the start of winter. Hm. I must do an article for the journal of ornithology, post haste, nothing but post haste can be enough haste. Yes. Yes. Yes. *(The PROFESSOR exits. The swallow opens her eyes and wipes something from her head. She looks up. Then she wipes a second time)*

SWALLOW. Worst climate on earth, Northern Europe. The air's cold and the rain's hot ... why ... why ... it's not rain ... It's coming from the ... How in heaven can a statue ... Is it crying or something? Hey, are you crying?

PRINCE. I'm sorry ... I ... I ... I suppose I am.

SWALLOW. Who are you?

PRINCE. I'm the Happy Prince.

SWALLOW. How can you be a happy prince if you're crying? I can't take a lot of paradox. I'm only a bird.

PRINCE. Accept my apology. Even though I have a heart of lead, what I see out there, the unhappiness, it affects me. *(He sniffs)* What's a swallow doing this far north? Winter's hand is about to smother us.

SWALLOW. If you must know I was stupid; that's what I'm doing here. I'm stupid. I fell in love with a warbler. Me. I've always thought I had more class than that. He told me I had the most slender waist and the shapliest legs of any bird on the continent. You know the kind of fluff birds fall for. And I fell for it all. Swooning and hanging upside down on tree limbs whistling off key. They all laughed at me. And this warbler, he just wanted to have a hot time summer romance. He wasn't sincere. After he finished with me he flew off with a blue jay with rich relatives. That's a cock for you. Now I'm wiser but my flock is probably at the pyramids by now. I've got to catch up and try to ... *(She wipes another of the PRINCE's falling tears)*

PRINCE. I'm sorry.

SWALLOW. Look, is there anything I can do?

PRINCE. Well...

SWALLOW. While I'm here. Go ahead tell me. I mean, you're putting out more water than a nimbus cloud, O Happy Prince.

PRINCE. *(After sniffing)* All right, listen, I can see not far from here through an open window a woman. A seamstress. She's hungry and tired.

SWALLOW. Aren't they all?

PRINCE. But she's got a son and he's sick in bed with fever. She's got so much work she can't even tend to him.

SWALLOW. Good God,no. Why is she sewing this late?

PRINCE. She's embroidering passion flowers for the Queen's maids of honor to wear at the next court ball. The last meal she or her son had was orange rinds and some river water.

SWALLOW. And how can I help them?

PRINCE. Take her the ruby out of my sword.

SWALLOW. It's a beautiful stone. Worth a fortune.

PRINCE. Yes, it'll buy her food and medicine for the boy. And when those in the palace — I know them well — come to mistreat her for not finishing her work, she'll be able to laugh in their faces.

SWALLOW. You talked me into it. *(Prying loose the stone)* The poor things. I should be gliding along the Nile eating the seeds of lotus flowers and I'm here freezing my tail off doing good deeds. Oh, I'm so easy. My heart simpers at anything. *(Getting the stone loose)* There. I'll be off now.

SOUL. *(Entering as the bird uses the stage as a runway and exits)* The swallow flew up over the cathedral and saw the whole country. She saw the noble women sipping wine and cursing the seamstress who they said never had her work done on time because she was lazy. Then with the ruby in her mouth she flitted through the window of the poor seamstress' house and dropped the ruby in her lap.

SEAMSTRESS' VOICE. *(Off)* A ruby! That bird! She left me a ruby!

SOUL. The swallow also cooled the boy's fever by the rapid flutter of her wings near his brow and then she flew back to the prince ... *(The SWALLOW enters tired and falls asleep at the foot of the statue)* ... tired, but as happy as her confederate with the heart of lead. *(SOUL goes off)*

PRINCE. Pssst! I say pssst!

SWALLOW. Huh? Who ... Who said pssst to me?

PRINCE. Up here.

SWALLOW. Oh. Good Lord, look at the sun. I've slept half the day away. Good, good, Lord.

PRINCE. I know. Some children came by and threw stones at you and that ornithologist sneaked up, pulled your wings way out and measured you.

SWALLOW. While I was asleep? My wings? The pervert!

PRINCE. I couldn't wake you.

SWALLOW. It was a long trip with that heavy ruby in my beak. I'm not used to hauling cargo, you know. I'm just a little swallow, not a carrier pigeon.

PRINCE. I wish you'd stay with me one night more.

SWALLOW. You've got to be kidding. I can't. I've got to leave for Egypt. The sphinx, the pyramids, the warm sand, the fig trees, the...

PRINCE. There's a young fellow in a garret. He's trying to finish a comedy for the local theater. But he's too cold to write any more. Maybe the two of us...

SWALLOW. I'd love to but my flock is probably pearched on the head of the great god Memnon waiting for me. So I can't possibly...

PRINCE. The cold and hunger have made him faint.

SWALLOW. Oh, no. I know how he feels. I'd faint myself but I have such a long trip and I just must...

PRINCE. But we can help him.

SWALLOW. We? Say, how'd I become half of this charity

team? All I did was stop here to rest my wings. The man chose to write for the theater. It's always chancy, show business. I'm sure he knows that; I'm sure he...

PRINCE. My eyes are made of rare sapphire. Pluck one out and take it to him.

SWALLOW. What? One of your ... one of your eyes? Dear generous friend, I could never do that.

PRINCE. You must do as I tell you. He is a writer of comedies, this man. Laughter keeps the world healthy. That's more precious than a sapphire. We must save him. Work quickly. I command it!

SOUL. *(Enters as the SWALLOW climbs up the pedestal)* It took her working gently using beak and claw and with tears in her eyes the whole afternoon to finally pry the jewel loose.

PRINCE. *(With one eye closed now)* Thank you, Friend. Don't worry about me. Fly to him now.

SOUL. *(As the SWALLOW exits)* Again she took the wind. She flew hard and sure to the clammy room of the playwright. The sapphire was even heavier than the ruby and she dropped it into the writier's ink well, waking him with splattering cold ink!

PLAYWRIGHT'S VOICE. *(Off)* It's magic!

SOUL. The writer was stunned with joy.

PLAYWRIGHT'S VOICE. *(Off)* It's a magical swallow who saved me with this rich gem!

SOUL. But the swallow was far from magical.

SWALLOW. *(Re-entering exhausted)* Magic, my foot! You stick the sapphire in your mouth and flap your wings to beat the band. Magical. Writers' fantasies, whew!

SOUL. *(AS SWALLOW curls up at the foot of the statue)* Even with the cold weather she slept deep into the next day.

PRINCE. *(As SOUL exits)*Little swallow! Little swallow!

SWALLOW. *(In her sleep)* The crocodile's in the mud...

PRINCE. Little Swallow!

SWALLOW. There's the temple of Boalbec and...

PRINCE. Swallow!!

SWALLOW. *(Waking)* Who? Oh ... It's you ... Well, my generous nobleman, today I must finally leave. I'm shivering. I can't feel my feet. Frost is coming, oh yes.

PRINCE. It's true, but you can stay one more night.

SWALLOW. It's winter, O great magnanimous Prince. I must got to Egypt and find a niche on a palm tree.

PRINCE. But in the square across town there's a match girl. Her matches have fallen into the gutter and they're now useless. Unless she comes home with money, her father will beat her. He beats the whole family. Give her my other eye.

SWALLOW. I will stay with you another night because ... because your heart is the most giving of any I have ever seen. But I won't peck and paw at your other eye

PRINCE. You must. You must listen to me.

SWALLOW. But, O lover of man, you'll be blind. No!

PRINCE. And if I keep this sapphire eye I will see a child beaten ... I command you as my friend to do this for me. There's no time to lose. Come up. Come up now! As a prince I command you! *(SOUL enters as the SWALLOW reluctantly climbs up on the pedestal)*

SOUL. Once more it took hours to work out the other rich eye from the Prince. *(ThePRINCE closes both eyes now)* But the Swallow persisted and the Prince coaxed and the eye came out.

PRINCE. *(As the SWALLOW exits)* Hurry! There's not much time! She's right behind the blacksmith's shop. Hurry!

SOUL. The Swallow flew against a strong wind with the heavy jewel and lighted on the shoulder of the match girl. Just as her father was about to open the door, the bird put the sapphire in her hand and her face came alive with wonder.

FATHER. *(Off)* Well, Girl, what've you earned today? Don't dawdle.

GIRL. *(Off as the SWALLOW slowly re-enters)* Father, a bird from heaven gave me this rich jewel. Surely now you are happy and can start loving us again.

SOUL. But the bird had not been sent by God.

SWALLOW. *(As SOUL exits)* She said I'd been sent by God, my Prince. Children. It made me feel good that she said so, though.

PRINCE. I've kept you too long. Rest now. In the morning when I feel the sun I'll wake you and you'll fly to Egypt.

SWALLOW. No. You're blind. I've got to stay with you now.

PRINCE. No, little swallow. You must go. The winter will...

SWALLOW. No. Flying back from the little girl's house I thought it all out. I will stay with you forever and be your eyes. Even if you command me I will disobey you, my Prince.

SOUL. *(Entering as the SWALLOW climbs up and whispers in the PRINCE's ear)* For days and days the Swallow told the

Happy Prince of all who passed and who bought what from the venders and how the writer's comedy went at the theater, of how the seamstress and her son who got well were doing. She told how happy, and now well-dressed the little match girl was. At night she told him of the mountains and the camels in Egypt and how the butterflies there were as big as a Duchess' fan. But there were no butterflies around here at all. The frost had killed them all. *(SOUL exits as two boys enter. They are shivering with cold)*

BOY 1. The Prince looks as cold as we do.

BOY 2. Yes, but he's not cold or hungry since he's made of metal. *(They go off)*

PRINCE. Precious little Swallow. I love your stories. It helps me forget the suffering of men and women. Since I can't convince you to go to Egypt, I want you to do something else for me.

SWALLOW. As you say it, I'll do it. I surely wish someone would build a fire around the square here though.

PRINCE. Not many can even afford firewood for their homes. Listen to me. There are strips of gold leaf decorating my cap and doublet. Take them off leaf by leaf and give them to the poor.

SOUL. *(Entering as the SWALLOW takes off each strip of gold leaf)* Piece by piece the bird peeled off the last dressing from the statue. It took two nights and two days for the swallow to get every last bit of the valuable metal. *(The SWALLOW exits with the gold)* Then she scudded about the town dropping the gold at the feet of the poor. *(A Carpenter and his wife run by holding a piece of gold)*

CARPENTER. It has to be from heaven! It's gold!

WIFE. You'll be able to keep your carpenter's shop now!

CARPENTER. It's a day to sing for joy, my Love!

ANOTHER MAN. *(Holding some gold enters as the Carpenter and his wife exit)* Gold! Gold! It's a miracle! Gold, I tell you!

NUN. *(Entering)* What is it? What's the matter?

MAN. *(Holding up his gold)* From the sky, Sister, Gold! I'm going to buy a new cow from the mayor so the children can have warm milk in the morning! Gold from the sky! *(The man runs off. The SWALLOW enters and comes up behind the nun)*

NUN. But, wait, I didn't see any … *(The SWALLOW drops a piece of gold over the nun's shoulder and exits)* Any … *(She picks it up)* Gold! It's gold! Yes, it is. From the sky just as he said. Now the convent will have firewood and food and we can take in some of the poor and … *(Two boys run on with loaves of bread)*

BOY 1. Would you like some bread, Sister? We have plenty.

BOY 2. Yeah, ain't you heard? Gold fell from heaven!

SISTER. No, I don't need any bread. But bless you for thinking of me. God answered my prayers too. See. *(She shows them her gold)* Praise God, Children. *(The boys and the sister wave and run off joyously shouting "Gold" as the SWALLOW returns exhausted and collapses at the foot of the statue. The others make the sound of church bells in the distance)*

SWALLOW. If you only could see this town, my Prince.

Why, they're all...

PRINCE. No need to wear yourself out further telling me. I could hear them all day, and the priest is still ringing the church bell.

SWALLOW. Right in the middle of his Mass I dropped your gold on his Bible.

PRINCE. Well, he can use it for firewood too. It's snowing. I can feel the flakes on my head.

SWALLOW. Yes. The streets are silver with it. Prince, oh generous Prince, I'm sorry, really I am, but I really must say goodbye.

PRINCE. Don't be sorry.

SWALLOW. I want to kiss you before I go.

PRINCE. Please do. It's another happiness that on top of all you've done for our town, you're finally going to sunny Egypt at last.

SWALLOW. *(Getting up with difficulty)* I'm ... I'm not... I'm not going to Egypt. I'm ... I'm going to the house of death. I'm going to...

PRINCE. *(As she kisses him)* House of...

SWALLOW. Yes ... It is time.

PRINCE. No, little friend. No...

SWALLOW. It's not a matter of choice, blind Prince. It's ... It's ... it's so cold. *(The SWALLOW falls at his feet)*

PRINCE. Friend to man? Friend to man? Where are you? Where? Oh, God, that I had my eyes back with which to cry ... Oh, God, just one tear, I beg you! How can she be allowed to die without tears?! *(Enter MAYOR and TOWN COUNSELOR in top hats and the PROFESSOR in mortarboard hat. The others continue with the sound of the bells)*

Town Counselor. The children are all out sledding, Mr. Mayor, and over there, look, ice skating.

Mayor. Yes, Counselor, the sick are being cared for and the poor have their bellies full, just as I promised. When I became mayor, I vowed that I'd change the face of this town, didn't I? And I did it.

Professor. But how shabby the Happy Prince looks, Mr. Mayor.

Mayor. Shabby indeed. The ruby has been stolen from his sword. His eyes are gone and he's lost all his luster.

Town Counselor. Looks more like a beggar.

Professor. And here is that Swallow I told you all about. Dead. Probably pulled up here lame; that's my judgment. I know birds better than anyone and I tell you a swallow can't live this far North.

Mayor. A dead bird in the town square. Mr. Counselor, tomorrow I want a proclamation read that will forbid birds to die here. Now that I've got the town the way I want it, I want to keep it that way.

Town Counselor. Yes, Sir, Mr. Mayor, first thing tomorrow.

Mayor. And have this statue melted down. Let's put up something really beautiful that befits a prosperous town.

Town Counselor. How about a statue of you, Mr. Mayor?

Mayor. Me? I don't know ... Well, if you both think there's enough brass there, I won't stand in your way. And, Professor, do have some of your students throw that dead bird in the garbage or something.

PROFESSOR. Oh, yes, Mr. Mayor. They do smell up the place fast.

SOUL. *(Removing his mortarboard hat as the other two walk off. The bells become slower now, more solemn)* But when God looked down on this town of contented people, he said to one of his angels, go there and bring me the two most precious things you can find. And the angel came down here and returned to the Almighty with a lead heart and a dead swallow from a garbage heap. And God said to the angel: You have chosen rightly. *(The lights fade slowly on the town square as we hear the bells for a few beats in the darkness)*

THE NIGHTINGALE AND THE ROSE

(A spot light comes up on SOUL again. In the dimness behind him, the others form the risers into a garden wall and a bench stage left. One of the actors stands stage right as a rose bush)

SOUL. *(As a boy with a mathematics book moans)* Excuse him. He's in love. *(The Boy flops on the bench)* He's supposed to be studying his mathematics, but love — the most difficult of equations — just won't let him. *(SOUL exits as lights come up full and a NIGHTINGALE in half mask, [female] and a LIZARD in half mask, [male] enter. She's chirping and he is flicking his tongue)*

NIGHTINGALE. What's wrong with him, Lizard?

LIZARD. You sing in this garden all the time of love, Nightingale. Don't you recognize the real thing when you see it?

NIGHTINGALE. He's only a schoolboy.

LIZARD. *(As the boy crosses to the wall)* Almost sixteen now. The boy you pined for all these years.

NIGHTINGALE. All these nights I've sung about him to the stars.

LIZARD. We know, and kept us awake.

NIGHTINGALE. So young. He's so young for the sorrow of love. Who's the girl?

LIZARD. Very mundane. The girl next door.

NIGHTINGALE. The girl next door. Isn't that so...

LIZARD. *Shhhhh!* He's calling to her.

BOY. Love of my life, please come to the wall. Hello.

GIRL. *(Leaning over the wall)* What is it that you want? I've got to go inside soon. I don't want to catch a chill.

BOY. Oh, I won't keep you. I just ... Well ... I want to ask ... Well...

GIRL. Ask me what? I haven't got all day.

BOY. Don't go, please. I just want to ask you if tomorrow night at the king's ball you ... you would dance with me.

GIRL. I don't know. I would have to know ... well ... that you really wanted to dance with me. That I was going to be something special. After all, my mother told me that dancing is the latch key to romance.

BOY. Then more than ever I want to dance with you,

hold you in my arms, let the music carry us wherever it will.

GIRL. Oh? Then ... then I will ... I will consider dancing with you ... if you bring me a ... a red rose, yes, a red rose.

BOY. A red rose?

GIRL. Yes, I'll have a pink dress and only red will do. I've got to go now. Goodbye. *(She goes off up stage)*

BOY. But wait! There are no ... red roses around here. *(He crosses to the actor playing the rose bush)* I have the only rose bush in this kingdom and it's ... *(He shakes the bush)* Without flowers! *(He crosses back to the bench and flops on it)* The musicians will play the little cries of love on their strings and I'll be all alone to dance with my aunt or something. But for one damned precious red rose! If I cannot have her, I won't dance at all.

LIZARD. How ridiculous!

NIGHTINGALE. Why ridiculous? What's so ridiculous about love?

LIZARD. Look at him practically weeping over the girl next door. Because he can't find a red rose. Look, it's as though his heart is going to break. For what? For this intoxicating emotion, love!

NIGHTINGALE. Lizards are not a bit romantic.

LIZARD. Look, others already love him. You, for instance, and he never even looks up when you fly by any more. He's only got his eye on that pale wisp of a thing who lives next door.

NIGHTINGALE. Those who love us are never as important as those who don't. Besides, he's a boy.

LIZARD. Well, you flap and flutter around here all you

please. I'm going to catch insects. *(Exiting)* Love! Love! The world's not about love. It's about survival. *(The NIGHTINGALE crosses and circles the sad school boy. Then she crosses to the rose bush. She shakes it. It wakens from its sleep)*

ROSE BUSH. Huh? Oh, what is it, Nightingale?

NIGHTINGALE. A rose. A red rose. I must have one.

ROSE BUSH. What?

NIGHTINGALE. Give me a red rose for this boy and I'll sing for you. You're the only one in the kingdom.

ROSE BUSH. I know, but winter has put chills deep in my veins and frost's made death of my buds. There won't be any roses for me this year.

NIGHTINGALE. I only want one. One simple beautiful red.

ROSE BUSH. You can still get yellow and white. They're all over the country side.

NIGHTINGALE. You don't understand. It's a matter of love. That boy's love. One red rose, Oh, please. I must get it for him or the girl next door won't dance with him. There must be a way.

ROSE BUSH. There is ... There is one way.

NIGHTINGALE. Well? ... Well, go on, tell me that way.

ROSE BUSH. It's a horrible way, Nightingale.

NIGHTINGALE. Tell me ... Tell me...

ROSE BUSH. No.

NIGHTINGALE. Do I look afraid? Do I? Tell me, Rose Bush.

ROSE BUSH. All right, Nightingale, if you want a red rose you must make music by the open eye of the moon. You must sing to me with your breast against a thorn.

You have to sing the whole night and the thorn must pierce your heart so that your life-blood flows into my veins and becomes mine.

NIGHTINGALE. That ... that high a price? Death?

ROSE BUSH. You asked me. You asked me and I told you. *(The BOY rises and wraps his cloak around him to keep away the chill. The NIGHTINGALE crosses to him, but he just ignores her, picks up his mathematics book and exits)*

ROSE BUSH. Why would you even consider your life for a rose? Huh? You who love life so much.

NIGHTINGALE. Love is life at it's height. Besides, what is the heart of a bird compared to his heart? *(She crosses to where the boy exited)* You will be happy, Boy. All I hope for in return is that you'll be a true lover to that girl. I can see her now all in pink with ... with a red rose of love on her breast.

ROSE BUSH. It's too high a sacrifice.

NIGHTINGALE. No. Now he only knows what's in books. But when he has love, he will know the world. Why are we waiting? The cold moon watches. *(She crosses back to the ROSE BUSH)*

ROSE BUSH. I can see your mind won't be changed. *(The NIGHTINGALE pushes her torso against the arm of the ROSE BUSH and begins to whistle a quick cheerful song. This whistling becomes slower and slower as she weakens)*

SOUL. *(Stepping on stage)* The whole brisk night the Nightingale sang with her breast pressed to the thorn. The moon leaned down to listen. And the thorn went in further and further sucking away her life blood. The bird's music at the start told of the first love of a boy and girl...

Rose Bush. Blood! More blood! Press closer! Press closer to the thorn or the moon'll be gone before the rose is done.

Nightingale. I will ... I will...

Soul. The music then told of the passion of man and maid ... and finally as the thorn pierced the little Nightingale's heart, she whistled the dirge of love that is perfected by death ... and so she gave up her life for ... *(As the NIGHTINGALE slumps over, the ROSE BUSH slowly opens its hand to reveal a red rose)* A blood red rose. A sweeter scented rose I never smelled.

Rose Bush. The most precious red rose this kingdom or any other will ever see. *(Enter the LIZARD. He sees the NIGHTINGALE and he crosses to the dead bird)* She's dead. It was her last wish on earth that the young man who lives here was to have her rose. It is her life. Her life-blood rose.

Lizard. Her life. Her poor life. She gave her life blood by the open eye of the moon? Her poor, poor life for ... *(He kisses the dead NIGHTINGALE)* Oh, the fool. If only you had the good sense of a Lizard, you'd by flying in the sun today. *(Exiting)* She always had the strangest outlook on life: Love. She saw life as love. The fools that love makes of some. *(The BOY enters wiping sand from his eyes. He puts his book down on the bench. He sees the bird. Slowly, he crosses to her)*

Boy. Why it's ... it's the little Nightingale. She kept me up all night with her endless chirping ... She's ... she's dead ... She's been around here for as long as I can remember. Too bad. She had such fine form when she sang ... although it meant nothing, it was pleasant and ...

(He sees the rose) Good God! How lucky I am! This old bush did have a bloom in it! What a marvel nature is! Wait'll my love sees this! *(He plucks the rose and runs to the wall)* Hello! Over here! Hello there! *(The GIRL appears at the wall)* Good morning to you.

GIRL. And good morning to you.

BOY. *(Holding the rose behind his back)* You said you'd dance with me tonight if I brought you a red rose: Well, here. *(He presents the rose to her)* Well? Have you ever seen any rose as red? Will you wear it next to your heart at the ball and tell everyone that I gave it to you?

GIRL. *(Handing back the rose)* I'm afraid it won't go with my dress now. I'm not wearing the pink gown. I'm wearing a blue with blue shoes and...

BOY. But ... you promised...

GIRL. I know. But the Chamberlain's son sent me this gold necklace. Mother said it would be wise to dance every dance with him.

BOY. Every dance?

GIRL. Yes ... well, don't pout at me like that. Everybody knows gold necklaces cost more than flowers.

BOY. You promised me and now you've gone back on it. You are untrue to your word.

GIRL. You're rude. You're just jealous because you're not a Chamberlain's son, because you have nothing, no silver buckle on your belt or gold coins in your pocket. Good day to you! *(She disappears up stage)*

BOY. *(Throwing the rose over the wall)* You can go trample this red rose in your fancy blue shoes for all I care! *(He crosses back to the bench and sits)* Good God what a silly thing love is. Yesterday I was swooning over her. Why on earth? Love is not half as useful as mathematics. *(As the lights fade)* Where was I? Yes. If a and b are classes, then a+b=b+a ... and if a and b are classes then axb=bxa and... *(SOUL steps out into a spotlight as others arrange the risers to represent two doorways on opposite sides of the stage. At stage left, the doorway represents an exit from the cottage of LITTLE HANS. At stage right the doorway represents an entrance to BIG HUGH's home. So in front of BIG HUGH's door other risers represent table and chairs and perhaps the mantle of a fireplace)*

THE DEVOTED FRIEND

SOUL. Tales about kind hearts always make the best stories and I suppose the man with the kindest heart I ever met was a farmer called Little Hans. *(HANS enters through his doorway. He mimes sowing seeds)* No one had a finer garden. In it he grew...

HANS. *(Naming the rows as he points)* Sweet Williams, Gilly-Flowers, Shepherd's Purses, Roses, Lilac Crocuses, Violets, Columbine, Ladysmock, Marjoram, Wild Basil, Cowslip, and Daffodils.

SOUL. And don't forget the Forget-me-nots.

HANS. And, oh yes, the Forget-me-nots. I forgot the Forget-me-nots. and in the back of my cottage are the fruit trees.

SOUL. *(As HANS continues sowing and BIG HUGH and his wife and two children, a boy and a girl, enter their cottage from the other door)* The whole town loved Little Hans and called him a friend. But his best friend was Big Hugh, the miller.

HUGH. *(At the table with a basket)* Beautiful, eh? *(They pantomime taking fruit from the basket and eating it)*

WIFE. I've never seen cherries so big.

BOY. Or plums.

GIRL. I'd rather smell the flowers.

HUGH. I never go by Little Hans' place without a basket to fill up. *(Miming emptying his pockets)* Here're more sweet cherries and some apricots.

GIRL. Why is it, Father, that you never give Little Hans anything in return?

HUGH. What?

BOY. We have hundreds of sacks of flour in the basement, a field full of cows, a flock of sheep, and a whole store house of...

HUGH. I give Little Hans much more than any material thing is worth. I give Little Hans true friendship, Children.

BOY. Oh.

GIRL. True friendship is priceless. Absolutely priceless.

SOUL. *(As HANS stands in his doorway shivering)* During Spring, Summer and Autumn, Little Hans sold his flowers and fruits to the townsfolks and he was happy. But when Winter dug its cold nails into the earth and froze it, the little farmer had nothing to sell. Later in Winter, he often had nothing to eat but some dried nuts. Most times it was too cold for him to sleep.

WIFE. *(As HUGH the miller and his family warm themselves*

by the fire) I wonder how Little Hans is faring in this wicked winter cold.

HUGH. *(Belching)* I think I ate too much.

BOY. I almost forgot all about Little Hans.

GIRL. Why don't we go see him, Father?

HUGH. What good would that do? All this snow is
trouble for everybody. And when people are in trouble,
Children, the last thing they need are visitors. In the Spring, I'll stop over to see him and he'll give me a big basket
of whatever's growing. That'll make him a happy
man.

WIFE. You certainly are thoughtful of others, Dear,
very thoughtful indeed.

BOY. Yes, he sounds like a clergyman.

GIRL. But we could ask Little Hans to come up here. If
he's in trouble I'd give him some of my porridge.

HUGH. What a silly girl. I don't know why I send you to
school. What do you learn? If I had Little Hans up here
and he felt this warm fire and saw the food and wine he'd
get envious. And there's nothing to destroy a man's soul
faster than envy. You think I'd have anything to do with
destroying my best friend?

GIRL. I never thought of it that way.

HUGH. Because you're young. I don't want to lead Little Hans into any temptation. If he came up here, surely,
hungry as he is, he'd probably be tempted to borrow a
sack of flour on credit. Flour is material, but friendship is
spiritual and eternal. Besides, credit is a step away from
taking something for nothing and the word for that
is...

BOY. Cheating.

Hugh. Indeed. You think I'd make a criminal out of my best friend, Little Hans? Never. I love him too dearly.

Wife. To hear a man talk like this is just like being in church, isn't it, Children?

Boy. Yes, Mother, I'm even getting drowsy. Good night.

Soul. *(As the Miller family all say goodnight to one another and exit and LITTLE HANS comes through his door way and simulates raking his garden)* When the painful winter finished and nature began to send flowers up to the world again, Big Hugh went down to see Little Hans.

Hugh. *(Enters with a basket)* Good morning, Little Hans.

Hans. Oh! Well, a very good morning to you, Big Hugh.

Hugh. Thank you. How lovely your primroses look. Mind if I take a few for the wife.

Hans. *(As HUGH puts the basket on HANS' arm and begins picking the primroses)* Not at ... all.

Hugh. *(As he mimes picking and putting flowers in the basket)* And how have you been all winter?

Hans. It's very good of you to ask. I had a tough time of it. But now that it's Spring and my flowers are growing so big...

Hugh. Quite big. We often spoke of you during the cold nights, you'll be very pleased to know.

Hans. How kind of you. I thought you forgot all about me.

Hugh. Don't ever say that about me, ever, Hans.

Hans. I'm sorry, I didn't mean...

HUGH. Friendship *never never never* forgets, Hans.

HANS. I'm so sorry. I really am, Hugh. I should've realized how good a friend you are.

HUGH. *(Taking the last flower in the row)* The family's going to love these primroses though and it'll sort of make up to them for you when I tell them that you said we forgot you. They're exceptional primroses.

HANS. They ... They ... certainly ... certainly are ... I ... I was going to take them to market and sell them and use the money to buy back my wheelbarrow.

HUGH. *(Rising and taking the basket from LITTLE HANS)* Buy back your wheelbarrow? Who would be so stupid as to sell his wheelbarrow?

HANS. I had to, Hugh. I had to buy bread. First, I sold the silver buttons off my coat to the blacksmith. Then I sold my pipe to the barber. Then my brass lantern to the tavern keeper. My wheelbarrow went to the lumberjack. But I'm going to buy them all back.

HUGH. Talk about coincidence. I just bought a wheelbarrow from the lumberjack. A beauty. Red with black wheels.

HANS. That's the one I sold him! What a coincidence indeed.

HUGH. I guess that's how the world works. We all do for each other. In some way we're all connected by deeds.

HANS. What a nice sentiment, Hugh.

HUGH. Yes, and what I'm going to do for you is this, Hans. I'm going to give you my old wheelbarrow. It needs some work. One side is gone and the spokes are crushed, but look, hey, it's yours.

HANS. It is?

HUGH. I know it's very generous of me and everyone'll think me a fool, but I'm not like everyone else. I think that generosity is the hand clasp of friendship. Besides, I have your new one for myself.

HANS. It's still very generous, very very generous of you. I'll repair the wheelbarrow. I have a plank of woods that the lumberjack threw in with the deal.

HUGH. You have a plank of wood? *(HANS nods yes)* You know, that's just what I need for my barn roof. It's developed a leak and I don't want the corn to get wet. Am I lucky you have a plank. You see, Hans, how one good action breeds another? I give you my wheelbarrow. You give me your plank. Oh, I know the wheelbarrow's worth more than the plank, but true friends never look at that. Get that plank for me, huh? I want to cover that hole as soon as possible.

HANS. Oh, sure, yes, my ... my ... my plank. Yes. *(He gets the plank and gives it to BIG HUGH)*

HUGH. Hmmm. It's not a very big plank, Hans. After I fix my roof, there won't be any wood left for you to mend the wheelbarrow ... Don't look that way. It's not my fault.

HANS. Oh, I'm not looking any way. All these primroses and a plank of wood would never repay you for your wheelbarrow and good will towards me.

HUGH. Don't mention it, Little Hans. Goodbye now.

HANS. Goodbye, Big Hugh. And I will mention it often.

SOUL. *(As the two exit)* The next day when Little Hans

was nailing up some honeysuckle behind the cottage, he heard the miller's voice call out:

HUGH. *(Off)* Hans! Say, Hans! Hello, Hans! Hans? *(LITTLE HANS enters from around the doorway)*

LITTLE HANS. Who's calling? Who is it? *(BIG HUGH enters struggling with a heavy sack of flour on his back)*

HUGH. Dear Little Hans, could you do me a favor? *(He drops the sack on the ground)*

HANS. Anything.

HUGH. Could you carry this little sack of flour to market and sell it for me?

HANS. Oh, my, I'm ... I've got my creepers to nail up and the honeysuckle are hanging without any...

HUGH. No kidding, Hans, I think considering that I'm giving you my old wheelbarrow, that you're being rude.

HANS. Oh, no, I don't mean to ... I wouldn't be rude to my best friend. Look, let me just carry it to market for you.

HUGH. I don't know. After the way you insulted me.

HANS. Please, Hugh. Please forgive me. Please.

HUGH. All right this time, but I wouldn't take it a second time.

HANS. There'll be no second time. No second time. No. *(LITTLE HANS struggles to pick up the sack. Then he exits, straining under the weight)*

HUGH. Don't drop it. I'll come all the way down here for the money tomorrow myself.

HANS. *(Off)* Oh, thank you, Hugh.

HUGH. *(Exiting)* Don't mention it. What's a good deed

between friends?

SOUL. It took Little Hans the whole afternoon to carry the heavy load to town and sell it. At sunrise the next day Big Hugh came down to get the money for his sack of flour. *(HUGH enters, looks around; then he knocks at HANS' front door)*

HUGH. Hans! Little Hans! It's me! Hans? Hey there, Hans?

HANS. *(Appearing in the doorway, sleepy)* Oh, my God! I overslept!

HUGH. You are really some lazy farmer, Hans.

HANS. I was just so tired from carrying that flour and waiting all day in line at market to sell it that I couldn't get up. But I, at least, got you a good price for your flour. Here. *(He hands BIG HUGH a purse of money)*

HUGH. As one friend to another, Hans, I tell you, I think you should push yourself a little harder. Idleness is a great sin. Look, I only say this because you're a friend and I don't want my friends known as lazy. Lazy Hans. There goes Lazy Hans.

HANS. Please, oh, please don't say that.

HUGH. What good is friendship if one can't say what's on one's mind? You don't want me to be a flatterer, do you, you sleepy headed log?

HANS. No. No. No. No. No.

HUGH. Anybody can flatter you, but a friend tells another friend the truth. I mean, if I'm not permitted to call you what you are then I'd rather not have you for a...

HANS. No! Cut me to ribbons when I err, Hugh. Your friendly advice awakened me. Now I'm steamed up to move mountains. Thank you, Hugh.

HUGH. I'm glad because I want you to come up to the mill and fix my barn roof.

HANS. Today? *(HUGH nods yes)* Well, I have so much here to do that ... Do you think it would unfriendly of me if I said I'd love to fix your roof but I was busy? *(HUGH nods yes)* You know why I like having you as a friend, Big Hugh? Because you keep me from one social blunder after another.

HUGH. Considering that I'm going to give you my wheelbarrow, it's not too much to ask you to fix the roof. But you can still refuse and I'll go off and break my back and do it myself and...

HANS. No. no. My God, what're friends for? Let's go right now.

SOUL. *(As the two cross to BIG HUGH's house, LITTLE HANS with his arm around BIG HUGH, who counts his money)* Little Hans worked all day mending Big Hugh's barn roof. At sunset, Big Hugh came out of his cool house to inspect Little Hans' work)

HUGH. *(Entering with an exhausted LITTLE HANS)* I'm surprised it took this long.

HANS. I know but it's done. A nice job if I don't say so myself.

HUGH. And what greater reward is there than the work done for others, huh?

HANS. it's a privilege to hear you talk because I don't think I could phrase things half as beautiful as you.

HUGH. They'll come to you. It takes effort, Hans. Right now you have mastered only the practice of friendship. Some day you will master the theory as well.

HANS. You think so?

HUGH. There's no question about it. Now that you've fixed the roof, you'd better go home and rest because I want you to drive my sheep to the mountain tomorrow.

HANS. Tomorrow? But I ... I ... I...

HUGH. What is it, Hans?

HANS. I ... Nothing ... I'll see you tomorrow then.

HUGH. Bright and early. As a favor, I'll send the children down with the terrier to wake you up.

HANS. The little dog whose bark is like a bite? Oh, thank you, Big Hugh. Thank you.

HUGH. *(As HANS exits)* Get on your way and don't mention it. Friends don't always have to mention favors.

SOUL. *(As HUGH exits also and other make the sound of sheep off)* Poor Hans was afraid to say a thing lest he lose his best friend. The next day Little Hans sheparded the flock into the mountain and he thought he finally could get back to his own gardens and trees. But each day of summer, Big Hugh got Little Hans to do some other chore or errand:

HUGH. *(Off)* The irrigation ditch, Hans.

HANS. *(Off)* Dug! *(Shouted as they move from various parts of the stage)*

HUGH. The stable.

HANS. All cleaned out, Hugh.

HUGH. The front porch really needs paint.

HANS. I'll get the brushes!

HUGH. The machinery has to be oiled.

HANS. Done!

HUGH. My carriage...

HANS. Finished!

HUGH. The storage shed, Hans...

HANS. Completed!

HUGH. The basement needs...

HANS. Accomplished!

HUGH. My trellises...

HANS. Nailed up, Hugh!

HUGH. The road to the house...

HANS. Cemented!

HUGH. The children's room...

HANS. Cleaned!

HUGH. All this paper work...

HANS. Signed!

HUGH. The bricks for the chimney...

HANS. Delivered!

HUGH. *(Off)* You sweat a lot when you work, Hans, I really and truly wish you didn't have the perspiration problem; I really do.

HANS. *(Off)* Thanks Hugh. I'm lucky you're my best friend and wish only the best for me.

HUGH. *(As he and LITTLE HANS cross the stage)* Could you rub my neck, Hans? I pulled a muscle straining to see if you were coming with the bricks for my fireplace. You took all your good time about it.

SOUL. *(As LITTLE HANS steps into his doorway and BIG HUGH exits)* Little Hans was always so tired at day's end that he let his own flowers and fruits go. He'd look at his unweeded gardens and console himself by thinking...

HANS. Hugh, the miller is my best friend. I mean, the man's going to give me his old wheelbarrow. That's an act of pure generosity. *(He disappears behind the doorway)*

SOUL. One night ... *(Lights dim. The others make the sounds of storm. The lights flash lightning)* ... in the worst weather of the fall, Little Hans was just dozing off after building Big Hugh a chicken coop, when Big Hugh ran up to Little Hans' house.

HUGH. *(Enters in rain coat and hat and carrying a lantern. He knocks)* Hans! Hans! Hans! Open the door! Hans? Haannns! *(HANS appears at the doorway sleepy)* Good God! Asleep already?!

HANS. I'm sorry. I hope you'll forgive me.

HUGH. Dear neighbor Hans, I've got a crisis, my friend. My little son fell off a ladder and hurt his ankle. He was up on the ladder inspecting the chicken coop that you built me.

HANS. I'll never forgive myself.

HUGH. I'm going to call the doctor but he lives so far away and it's such a bad night — look at that lightning — that I thought it would be better if you went to call him, Hans.

HANS. Certainly. It's the least I can do since your boy was inspecting my work on the coop. I take it as a compliment, Hugh, that in time of crises you came to me.

HUGH. I do what I can for the people I'm devoted to, Hans.

HANS. *(Grabbing hat and rain coat)* Listen, I never really made enough money this year to buy back my lantern from the tavern keeper. If you could just lend me your lantern. *(Pause)* Huh? ... Hugh?

HUGH. I'm sorry, Hans, but this is my brand new lantern and I'd miss it if anything happened to it.

HANS. Oh ... Okay, even though it's a dreadful night I

think I can get to the doctor's. Don't worry. And Hugh...

HUGH. Yes, yes, what? Stop wasting time, Hans. It's my only son's ankle.

HANS. *(Getting on rain coat and hat)* I just wanted you to again know I appreciate your coming to me.

HUGH. In times of crisis is when friendship shines brightest. Don't ever feel you have to bring it up again, Hans. Go now, go.

SOUL. *(As the two go off in opposite directions)* The night was lucky and unlucky for Hans: He was lucky that two mile long bolts of lightning just missed his head. But with no lantern, he couldn't see where he was going, and, unluckily, he fell into a pond and drowned. *(The others wheel in LITTLE HANS, laid out on a riser used as a bier. All gather around mourning with flowers)*

HUGH. Since I was his best friend, it's only fair that I be first to lay the first flower.

WIFE. It's a good thing there were still a few left on Hans' place.

WOMAN. We're going to miss him around town.

BOY. Little Hans is a great loss to us all.

HUGH. A great loss to me for sure. Why, I had as good as given him my wheelbarrow.

GIRL. What are you going to do with that old wheelbarrow now, Father?

HUGH. I don't know. It's just in the way in my shed, and it's so broken down I'm sure I couldn't get anything for it. No. I'm never giving anything away again because ... *(As he places a flower on LITTLE HANS)* ... one always suffers for being generous.

SOUL. *(Staying in a spot as the lights fade on the mourners)* It's always dangerous to do a play with a moral, and that's why *The Devoted Friend* ends without one, just leaving you and your good sense to sort it all out ... later though, because it's time for my fisherman's play.

THE FISHERMAN AND HIS SOUL

(The lights come up dim on stage where the others are making the sound of waves breaking on the shore as they form the risers into a boat, stage right)

SOUL. *(As lights come up slowly and we see the FISHERMAN pulling in his net)* Every day my Fisherman went out to sea and made a good living in the marketplace with his catch. One evening ... *(SOUL exits)*

FISHERMAN. *(Laughing)* What in the name of the almighty could be making the net so heavy? *(Struggling)* It must be some sea monster or Neptune himself or ... *(He pulls the net from off stage. In it is a mermaid fighting the confines of the net)* For the love of...

MERMAID. Don't touch me!

FISHERMAN. Who ... What are...

MERMAID. I'm the daughter of a sea king.

FISHERMAN. You're beautiful.

MERMAID. I'm a mermaid. You must let me go. Do you hear me? *(Pause)* You must let me go back to the sea. *(One of the others, off, makes the sound of a horn)*

FISHERMAN. What was that?

MERMAID. One of the Tritons sounding the alarm.

FISHERMAN. Where do you live, Beauty of the sea?

MERMAID. Lower the net. You must.

FISHERMAN. Tell me where you live. Tell me what it's like. Please.

MERMAID. I live in a palace of pearl and amber. My bedroom overlooks a garden of coral fans. I was in that garden playing with the silver fish when your net snared me. You have to let me go back.

FISHERMAN. I ... I want to. I want to but ... I ... I can't.

MERMAID. Can't? Why not?

FISHERMAN. Because the sea has made your beauty magical, and the magic has made me love you. I won't rest until you be my bride.

MERMAID. Your bride?

FISHERMAN. Yes, I love you.

MERMAID. I couldn't be your bride.

FISHERMAN. Why not?

MERMAID. It's forbidden.

FISHERMAN. Your love's forbidden to me?

MERMAID. To men. You have a soul. For a man to have me he must rid himself of his soul.

FISHERMAN. Who said this?

MERMAID. It's the law of land and sea.

FISHERMAN. What use is a soul if it robs a man of you.

MERMAID. I told you. I'm forbidden. Now let me...

FISHERMAN. But I'll get rid of my soul and you'll be my bride. and in the pearl palace we'll be together. You can show me all the mysteries of the sea gods. I'm trapped in the net of your beauty just as you're trapped in my net of rope.

MERMAID. If then you would free me, as your reward I would marry you, Fisherman.

FISHERMAN. You will? You promise?

MERMAID. It's the only way I can go back to the sea, so, yes, I promise ... Well? I made a vow to you so you can let me go. Besides, if a man gave up his soul for me I would truly love him even though it is a crime against the sea gods to love a man. When your soul is gone, blow this. *(She hands him a conch shell)* When I hear the sound, I'll come.

FISHERMAN. But how do I rid myself of my soul?

MERMAID. I don't know. Those from the sea have no souls. *(He releases the rope and she slinks off the boat into the darkness. The lights fade and come up stage left. A priest sits at a riser on which is a small cross and he reads breviary. The FISHER-MAN enters)*

FISHERMAN. Father.

PRIEST. Ah, the town fisherman. How can I help you?

FISHERMAN. Something magical and strange but beautiful has happened.

PRIEST. Do tell me about this magical and strange but beautiful happening.

FISHERMAN. I ... Father, listen to me ... I fell in love with ... with one of the sea folk. *(The PRIEST rises)* I love her above all, but I can't have her as a bride until I rid myself of my soul.

PRIEST. Kneel down, Fisherman! *(The FISHERMAN*

kneels. The PRIEST blesses him) What force of evil paralyzes one of God's children? Let that force be gone in the name of the savior!

FISHERMAN. Father, you don't understand. I love her.

PRIEST. Are you crazy? Your soul is the noblest mark of man. Nothing is so precious as your soul. Get this thought from your mind.

FISHERMAN. She's all beauty and pleasure and desire and I...

PRIEST. Fisherman! The sea-folk are all lost. They are as beasts. The Lord didn't die for such as those.

FISHERMAN. Father, please help me. *(Rising)* The body lives fine without a soul. The sea folk are happy.

PRIEST. The body without its soul is cursed.

FISHERMAN. What good is it to have my soul if it keeps me from the one I love, Father?

PRIEST. God allows vile unnatural things in the world as temptation. Look at me. Look. Don't you think late at night, when I can't sleep, I haven't heard the Tritons blowing their horns in the sea trying to lure me from my prayers. They're lost. For them there's no heaven. No purgatory. Not even any hell. Just their eternal pagan sea.

FISHERMAN. You don't understand, Father. I snared the daughter of a king. For this daughter I'd give my soul. I would surrender heaven. Tell me how to sever this useless soul that keeps lovers apart.

PRIEST. Go home and pray to forget her. She is lost and you'll be lost with her. *(As the FISHERMAN runs off)* You'll be lost if you don't forget her! *(The lights fade on the PRIEST stage left. Others set risers up, stage left, to similate merchant's stands as SOUL enters and addresses the audience)*

SOUL. The sad young fisherman, not being able to stand the priest's eyes meet his, trundled down to the market. *(Two males and one female enter as MERCHANTS)*

MERCHANT 1. Rugs, buy rugs here!

SOUL. No thank you, just brousing. *(He goes off)*

MERCHANT 2. Precious gems! Special today! Gems!

MERCHANT 3. Spices! Spices from the Orient! Spices here!

FISHERMAN. *(Entering)* Hello all.

MERCHANT 1. Look who it is. Our friend the fisherman.

MERCHANT 2. Your stall is empty. No fish to sell?

FISHERMAN. Not today. But I'll sell you my soul.

MERCHANT 3. Your soul?

MERCHANT 2. He's kidding you. *(They laugh)*

FISHERMAN. No, I will. I'll sell any of you my soul.

MERCHANT 1. He's serious. but what use is a man's soul?

MERCHANT 3. It's not worth silver. Not my silver anyway.

MERCHANT 2. I would buy your body for a slave, but not a soul...

FISHERMAN. How strange. The priest tells me that the soul's worth all the gold in the world and they offer me nothing for it. *(As lights fade and the FISHERMAN exits)*

MERCHANT 1. Rugs! Buy rugs here!

MERCHANT 2. Precious gems! Special today!

MERCHANT 3. Spices! The finest from the Orient! Spices here!

SOUL. *(Stepping out of the darkness into a spot)* The Fisherman knew what he had to do. He knew right from the start. He fooled himself by not going straight away to the cave of witches in the hills. *(SOUL goes off and the lights come up stage right where the risers have been made into a cave entrance. A WITCH sits looking at the palm of her hand)*

FISHERMAN. *(Off)* Is anyone here?

WITCH. Come in, Fisherman. You'll have to crawl.

FISHERMAN. *(Crawling through)* How'd you know it was I?

WITCH. I could see it in my palm, Boy. Don't look so surprised. You came here for my cunning, didn't you?

FISHERMAN. Is there anything you don't know?

WITCH. Only what's on your mind. What do you lack, Boy? Huh? Fish for your net? I can fill it. But there's a price. What do you lack? A storm to wreck ships and leave their treasures to us? I can do it. At a price I can do it. What do you lack, huh? With my art, Boy, I can draw the moon from the sky or show you the face of death. What do you lack? Huh? Tell me your desires, my pretty boy, and I'll give them over — but you'll have to pay me a price.

FISHERMAN. It's not a great thing that I want. Yet the priest drove me away and the merchants mocked me. I come to you even though they call you and your sisters evil. As for the price, just name it.

WITCH. And the thing you want, my handsome one?

FISHERMAN. I want to be rid of my soul.

WITCH. Ohhh. Ohhh! My pretty one, this is a horrible

thing to do. No!

FISHERMAN. I want to be rid of it. I'll give you what gold I've saved and my nets, my house, my land, even my boat.

WITCH. *(Cackling)* I can turn leaves to gold or make silver out of moonbeams. The one I serve is richer than all the kings on earth.

FISHERMAN. What can I give you then?

WITCH. You can ... yes ... you can dance with me.

FISHERMAN. Is that all?

WITCH. That's a lot, pretty fellow. Dance with me and I'll tell you how to cast out your soul. Of course a few will watch us dance, my sisters and...

FISHERMAN. And whomever you want. Let's just get on with it. My love waits in the sea.

WITCH. Ah ... A sea-folk. Now I understand. I thought I saw in my palm the fork of Neptune. *(Two other witches crawl inside the cave)*

SISTER 1. Finally, the fisherman's going to dance with her!

FISHERMAN. How did they...

SISTER 2. We know!

SISTER 1. We know!

ALL THREE. We know!

FISHERMAN. Then let's go to it and...

WITCH. One other witness. *(A man in a crimson mask crawls inside. He wears gloves and a wide brimmed hat)*

FISHERMAN. Who ... Who is ... How did he find out about ... *(The witches put their fingers to their lips for the FISHERMAN to be silent. The three hags all kiss the man's hand. The strange man signals them to begin)* Is this the ... the...

WITCH. We call him ... the prince. Are you here to dance or talk, pretty one? *(The sisters begin clapping their hands and stomping their feet. The WITCH puts her arms around the FISHERMAN)* Am I not as fair as she from the sea? Take a good look.

FISHERMAN. No. *(They begin to dance to the clapping of the sisters faster and faster until the FISHERMAN finally stops)*

WITCH. Now kiss me.

FISHERMAN. No. You said a dance. And now it's done.

WITCH. One more dance and you'll beg to kiss me.

SISTER 1. Yes! Another dance!

SISTER 2. Dance again.

WITCH. Dance until we become as red as sunrise.

FISHERMAN. The pact we made said we would dance and we have.

STRANGE MAN. True, I heard the pact. But it couldn't hurt anyone to dance with her again.

FISHERMAN. My hungers are as strong as yours. Go away and let her tell me the secret of cutting off my soul. *(Pause)* Go. Go or I'll make the sign of the cross and if you are what I know you are your bodies'll spasm in pain like a fish out of the salt water.

(Pause, then he raises his hand to his forehead) In the name of the Father ... *(The sisters and the stranger scramble out of the cave in panic. The FISHERMAN grabs the WITCH and bends her to her knees)*

WITCH. Loose my arm! Loose me, I say!

FISHERMAN. No! My part is done! I've danced your black dance for you! Let's have your half! Tell me the secret! Tell me or I'll kill you for being a false witch! Tell me!

WITCH. So be it! *(He lets her arm go)* It's your soul, Boy. Here. *(She hands him a knife)*

FISHERMAN. What's this?

WITCH. A knife with a handle made of viper's skin. On the rocks of Neptune's shore use this to cut away your midnight shadow.

FISHERMAN. Cut away my...

WITCH. Yes. The shadow of the body is the body of the soul. Now you know the secret. So leave me alone. *(He takes the knife and crawls out as the lights fade and we hear the sound of the Tritons' horns off and the others making the sound of the sea and surf. A spot comes up left. Risers are strewn about representing rocks. The FISHERMAN barfooted with his pants rolled up enters. He has the conch shell in one hand and the knife in the other)*

FISHERMAN. I can feel her close to me. She's in the shallows beyond these rocks waiting. I feel it. *(He takes the knife and slowly carves away his shadow at his feet)* Let me now be free of you! The Tritons blow for me and my love. *(The horns play a single last note as SOUL steps out of the darkness. The FISHERMAN jumps)*

SOUL. You should've been frightened when you took that knife. Not at me.

FISHERMAN. You ... You ... You're the soul that's kept me from her?

SOUL. I've kept you from nothing. What evil have I done you that you discard me like this?

FISHERMAN. None. I feel odd being separated from you. I feel ... I feel alone. If ... If I didn't have her, I'd ... I'd kill myself now. I must call to her. *(He puts the conch shell to his lips)*

SOUL. Wait!

FISHERMAN. Don't touch me! The world said our love's forbidden when you're part of me!

SOUL. I'm afraid. I'm afraid, dear Fisherman, for you.

FISHERMAN. We must be apart, you and me. Leave me. I have no need of your concern.

SOUL. The sea gods won't protect you or her.

FISHERMAN. She made a vow to me.

SOUL. One the sea gods know she should've died before making. The horns, you heard the warning.

FISHERMAN. The tritons blew in celebration. Don't touch me! My heart is all love and I follow that love wherever it leads me.

SOUL. *(As the FISHERMAN blows the shell horn)* No! *(He blows it a second time and from behind one of the risers, in a spot light, the mermaid appears. the FISHERMAN crosses to her. They embrace and kiss)* If you love him, Lady of the Sea, send him back to me!

MERMAID. But I've waited for him.

FISHERMAN. And now she's my bride forever.

SOUL. Save him!

FISHERMAN. Ignore him!

MERMAID. After all he's given up for me, I can't...

FISHERMAN. Turn away from him! *(The embrace again. Then as the triton horns sound ominously the two lovers exit and the spot light on them fades and the horns again stop)*

SOUL. Fisherman! Fisherman! Come back! Can you hear me?! Fisherman! Nothing should separate a man and his soul! Can you hear me! Nothing should...

PRIEST. *(Enters)* It is so then? It's true what those hags

are saying? Has the Fisherman gone to that temptation from the sea?

Soul. Yes, Father. Yes, he's gone. No one could stop him.

Priest. Who are you?

Soul. A friend. I ... I came to disuade him, but he and she ... they ...

Priest. Where? Where, man?

Soul. Out there, Father. Beyond the rocks.

Priest. It's as black as sin. I see nothing.

Soul. Slipped beneath the waves both of them.

Priest. God forgive him his weakness.

Soul. He said it was love.

Priest. And I say again it is forbidden, whatever it is. *(He exits)*

Soul. *(As the lights slowly come up right to reveal the FISHERMAN and the MERMAID dead on the rocks)* Their bodies were found the next morning on the rocks by the inlet. Some children called the priest who came down from his church. *(Enter PRIEST)* His judgment on the two lovers was as clear, uncomplicated, and punctilious as was expected from a man of his station in life.

Priest. Never again will I bless these waters. Accursed are the sea folk and all who fall to their temptation. As for him who gave up heaven for this love, let him and his leman be buried under the rocky earth at Fuller's Field where nothing grows. No grave stone. No sign of any kind to mark their resting place. Let no one here dare mention them again. Accursed in life. Accursed also in death. It is only just. God protect us. *(SOUL crosses down center into a spotlight as the PRIEST exits and the lights fade behind him)*

SOUL. The grave diggers made the hole deep and tossed in the two lovers. No prayer was said. No tear fell. But in spite of what the priest commanded, every spring, in the place where nothing grows, white flowers stand up through the hard rocks of Fuller's Field over the earth where the Fisherman and his love lay entwined. And as the wind from the sea blows in, it carries the sweet smell of those flower cups to the entire town. The yearly occurence remains for the people who live there a thing of wonder and, for some, a thing of joy. *(The lights come up dimly in the background where the others set up a throne room)* I'm almost finished now spinning tales and working off the hapless Fisherman's penance. Yes, this fantastical world of Oscar Wilde concludes now with the story of *The Young King.*

THE YOUNG KING

SOUL. The old King's daughter had run off with an Italian. The old King was so angered that he had the swarthy Italian hunted down and killed. His daughter took their only son and fled to live with a farmer until she died of a broken heart. Years later when the dying King heard of this boy, his grandson, lived with peasant farmers, he had him brought to the palace to be crowned the new King. *(The lights come up full on the throne room. Attendants dress the young King and fuss with his hair and manicure his nails)*

TAILOR. Which tunic would your highness like?

YOUNG KING. Silk. Silk. Yes, a silk one.

TAILOR. All your tunics are silk, your Highness.

YOUNG KING. That's so. I'd almost forgot. The green one then. It'll match this turquoise ring that my grandfather gave me. And I'll wear my ivory-handled sword.

MANICURIST. You're going to look as if you stepped out of paradise at the coronation, Highness.

BARBER. I hear the robe is tissued gold cloth.

TAILOR. And word has it the gold crown's to be studded with rubies.

MANICURIST. And the grapevine says a body wouldn't be able to count all the pearls on the scepter.

YOUNG KING. Will you all stop saying you heard or word has it or the grapevine says. You all sneaked a look in the upper rooms where they're making everything. Admit it. Admit it now.

ALL. Yes your Highness.

YOUNG KING. It's all right. I won't punish any of you. It makes my heart skip to see myself on the altar of the great cathedral. Me. Me in the garb of royalty to accept the crown. Look around you.

MANICURIST. Yes, your Highness?

YOUNG KING. Stop combing my hair. Look at the tapestries, the gold, the cut venetian glass, the carved onyx, the silver inlaid ceiling. Look. Look out the window at the dome of my cathedral. My God, even the singing of the birds and the scent of the flowers seem to be mine.

BARBER. Not seem, are yours, Highness.

MANICURIST. Yes, your Highness.

TAILOR. Who else would they belong to?

YOUNG KING. That's true. Yes. Who else would they belong to? Go. Go now all of you and let me rest. *(The others exit. The young KING lies down on a riser and falls asleep. The lights dim as others enter and pantomime weaving cloth on a loom and making the sounds of battens falling and pressing threads together. They are tired and exhausted. SOUL is foreman)*

FOREMAN. You'll have to work faster and later tonight ... The young King's attendants must be dressed in silver clothes. It's his order. So don't look that way at me. You, make those stitches tight. And you, you'll all have to work faster. Faster, all of you.

YOUNG KING. *(Waking up)* What is it? Who ... who are ... who are you?

FOREMAN. I'm the foreman at this cloth factory, Sir.

YOUNG KING. Factory?

FOREMAN. This is a factory for making the finest cloth.

YOUNG KING. Oh. Then I must be passing through your life in my dreams. I just fell asleep at the palace where I'm to be...

FOREMAN. The palace? Are you a spy from our master?

YOUNG KING. Who's your master?

FOREMAN. Who? Why he's a man just like these but the difference is that he wears gold robes while we go in rags. He eats full belly every meal while we feel pangs.

YOUNG KING. The land is free and you people aren't slaves.

WEAVER 1. *(Laughs)* We're slaves and they call us free.

FOREMAN. In war the strong make slaves of the weak. In peace the rich make slaves of the poor.

WEAVER 2. We work to live.

WEAVER 3. But they give us such wages that we die.

WEAVER 4. We work 'till late at night and they heap gold in their pockets.

WEAVER 5. Our children fade away before their time.

WEAVER 1. And become hard and evil.

WEAVER. We tread the grapes while others drink the wine.

WEAVER 3. We sow, they reap. *(Others all agree to all that's been said)*

YOUNG KING. Is it so with everyone in the kingdom?

FOREMAN. Sure it is. The merchants make us earn their pay. The priest remember us in his beads and goes by. Poverty and sin lick each other's faces. Misery wakes us in the morning and gloom puts us to bed at night. But what could you care, you're young and rich from the palace.

YOUNG KING. What ... what cloth is this you're making?

FOREMAN. It's for the coronation. Gold cloth for the young King, silver for the attendants. What's it to you?

YOUNG KING. *(As SOUL puts on a sailor's hat and takes a whip and the others move a few risers to form a boat and begin to pantomime rowing)* What're you doing? ... I say, what're you all doing? Where ... Where are we going? Answer me.

Foreman. I say, Foreman, what...

CAPTAIN. *(As others grunt with effort)* I'm a captain, Sir. Captain of the ship here.

YOUNG KING. Captain of ... Why are these men in chains, Captain?

CAPTAIN. They're slaves, Sir. Chains are their badges, so to speak, Sir. Keep these oars movin'! We're late as it is! Put your backs into it! Or I swear I'll put the lash into your backs!

YOUNG KING. Where are we going?

CAPTAIN. To the spot, Sir, aye, the spot. Big oyster, big pearl.

YOUNG KING. Pearl?

CAPTAIN. The young King's scepter is being lined with pearls and they need one big one to cap the top of it. *(He points to one of the rowers)* We were at the spot yesterday. He — *he* — this one couldn't keep his breath long enough to reach the depth, Sir. *(Holding up the whip)* Fifty of these showed the others how to make the air last a little longer in the lungs. This is the spot! Stop! Anchor! *(One of the rowers pantomimes throwing the anchor over. Another makes the sound of it splashing into the water. A diver stands. He has a rope aroung his leg)* The big oyster, the big pearl or you get what he got. *(He pushes the slave-diver off the back of the boat. The diver disappears behind the riser. Others hold the rope as it unravels. The CAPTAIN and the young KING watch)*

YOUNG KING. What's so important about a pearl that men are made to suffer so?

CAPTAIN. What's so important? Everyone in the kingdom knows why it's important, Sir. The young King's scepter is to be ringed with fine quality pearls and

I told you they need a big one for the cap. It's my job to see that we came into port today with the right size pearl. It's quite a job to open one of those huge shells.

YOUNG KING. How will he stay down there so long?

CAPTAIN. It's either a blistering lung or a blistering back. The trick is to make him know that his back'll feel worse than his lungs. That's how you get the job done. But don't worry, Sir. Just you sniff in these wonderful sea breezes here. It'll do wonders for your appetite, Sir. *(The others begin pulling in the rope)* Want to see a top quality pearl, Sir? Step this way. *(The others pull the diver on board. In his hand is a large pearl)* You see. He's got it.

ROWER 1. It's a beauty, Sir. He's cut up a bit, but he brought back a beauty.

ROWER 2. Flawless, Sir.

CAPTAIN. Ah, I wish I could keep it myself.

YOUNG KING. But how is this diver? How is he?

ROWER 3. He's dead, Sir.

YOUNG KING. Dead?

ROWER 4. Anybody can see that he is. Sharks or something, Sir.

CAPTAIN. All right, don't stand there and gawk! Throw him overboard and let's get this beauty back to the King's jeweler. *(They throw the dead man over)* Would you like to hold it a minute, Sir?

YOUNG KING. No! Never! I want to wake up now. I want to be rid of this dream! *(The lights dim. The Young KING runs from the boat as the others move the boat risers away and begin pantomime digging. SOUL puts on a dark cloak and faces upstage. The lights come up brighter)*

MAN IN BLACK. *(To the diggers)* It won't be long now. I

mean, you have that to look forward to. It won't be too much longer.

YOUNG KING. *(Crossing to SOUL)* What won't be too much longer? Who are you?

MAN IN BLACK. Nobody. Nobody. I'm just waiting for them.

YOUNG KING. What are they doing? Why are they digging when they're so pale and sickly?

MAN IN BLACK. You must've wandered in too far, Sir. This is a mine. These people dig for rubies, Sir.

YOUNG KING. Digging for rubies?

MAN IN BLACK. Yes. Rubies. It takes a long time just to find one. You know how many an artist needs for a king's crown?

YOUNG KING. No.

MAN IN BLACK. Too many.

YOUNG KING. Regardless, these people are too ill to go on. You said they only had a short time.

MAN IN BLACK. *(Turning to the Young KING. He is wearing a death mask)* They do. None of them here will live out this day. It won't be much longer.

YOUNG KING. *(Running back to his bed and lying down)* No! No! No! No! *(He tosses and turns as SOUL and the others march off stage. Then he awakens with a start)* Good Lord, what dreams! *(The attendants enter with gold robe, pearled scepter and ruby-studded crown)* What's this?

ATTENDANT 1. Your robe, your Highness.

ATTENDANT 2. Your scepter, Highness.

ATTENDANT 3. Your crown, Highness. *(SOUL enters wearing bishop's mitre and a cross around his neck)*

BISHOP. It's time for your coronation. You must get

ready.

YOUNG KING. *(Rising)* Take these things away from me. I won't have them. Bring me the clothes I wore when I came to the palace ... Now! *(One of the Attendants exits)*

BISHOP. Your Highness, the coronation. The people wait.

YOUNG KING. Bishop, I won't wear this ... *(He touches the robe)* ... made from the loom of sorrow. Or carry this ... *(He hands the BISHOP the scepter)* ... stained with blood pearls. *(He gives the crown to the BISHOP)* Or own this, rife with the jewels of death.

BISHOP. But why?

YOUNG KING. Something is wrong when a man's dream becomes a journey of horror. My dreams made me see all. The hardship of men to make these.

BISHOP. Dreams? But, you Highness, dreams are not real. We don't heed dreams.

YOUNG KING. No man's dream can be false. I have seen the lives of those who toil for us and I tell you I'll have none of it, none of it, Holy Man.

BISHOP. *(As Attendant enters with old tunic, sandles and wooden staff)* All of you leave me alone with his Highness. *(The Attendants all exit)* Your Highness, the people wait for the coronation of a king. What have we to do with the lives of those who toil for us? It's their work. Lighten your mind. Put on this magnificent robe of gold. Set the crown on your royal brow. How shall the people know you stretch from a whole line of kings if you don't look like a king?

YOUNG KING. If a man could be a king by his costume then my barber could rule, Bishop. *(He puts on the old tunic and sandles and takes the wooden staff)* These I had when they found me tilling the soil.

BISHOP. The King is dead and the people wait for their new King. Who will rule if...

YOUNG KING. I didn't say I wouldn't rule. I said I wouldn't live this life of luxury.

BISHOP. From out of your grand living comes the little life of the poor. By your pomp their empty lives are nurtured. Your extravagances give them bread. Who'd feed them otherwise?

YOUNG KING. Aren't the rich and the poor brothers?

BISHOP. Of course, but the rich are rich brothers. And our crumbs are their manna from heaven, your Highness. Please, put on the robe. The coronation mass is about to...

YOUNG KING. I won't wear what grief has fashioned.

BISHOP. Son, I am now old and I've seen also. Oh, I know there're evils in the world: Robbers who sell children to the Moors, pirates who pillage, lepers who roam the marshes, beggars who fight dogs for scraps, and on and on. But what can we do? Will you have a leper in the palace? Will you give every beggar and tramp a place at your table? Will you sip wine with thieves? Doesn't only God know why these miseries exist? Of course. The sorrows of the world are too great for one heart to suffer.

YOUNG KING. You who wear his cross say that?

BISHOP. Your Highness you must listen to...

YOUNG KING. May I borrow your cross?

BISHOP. *(Giving him his cross)* You may borrow anything I have if only you'll take this now and ... *(He tries to hand the*

Young KING the robe)

YOUNG KING. Have this robe cut up and given to the poorest families to make clothing for their children. *(He takes the crown)* Have this melted down and build a school. *(He lays down the pearled scepter)* And sell these pearls and build a hospital. These are commands from the King.

BISHOP. Commands from ... Yes, your Highness.

YOUNG KING. *(Puts the cross around his neck)* Now I'm ready. Now my conscience is clear enough to meet the people.

BISHOP. Yes, your Highness. This day a greater power than I has already crowned you King in your heart. I beg of you, young King, teach us all what your dreams have taught you. *(The young KING kneels and kisses the BISHOP's ring; then he rises and exits. SOUL removes the mitre and crosses down stage to the audience)*

SOUL. The people took to the young King as they had never taken to the old. *(Others carry the young KING on behind SOUL, all cheering "Long live the young King!")* They carried him through the towns and villages and his face became as radiant as an angel's. His subjects dubbed him, this young man, the King of love, for while he reigned his only proclamation to farmers, tradesmen, millers, woodcutters, fishermen, princes, dukes, nobles of all kinds, orphans, clergy, yes, to the whole of man, was human compassion. And the people he ruled over were happy, happy beyond the happily ever after of fairy tales even. Their souls were at one with them all, and they remained so, until the day that King died ... *(The lights fade on SOUL as he joins the others in their cheer for the new King)*

— END —

PRODUCTION NOTES

1.   If plays are being done individually, the character of Soul simply becomes a narrator, and any line that he has that refers to him as Soul is just changed or cut. For instance, in *The Birthday of the Infanta,* the narrator might start the play by saying, "Good evening, Ladies and Gentlemen, Tonight we invite you to a birthday party. A special birthday party, the birthday party of a princess, the Infanta of Spain. I am the guardian of this little princess here, etc." The play then concludes with Don Pedro's last line: "Yes, dear one, I can understand that ... anyone could."

With a few minor adjustments like this, all the plays will work as single units.

2.   In scenes where there are animals, except where masks are specifically called for, no attempt should be made to literally make the actors look like animals. The dialogue will be enough to identify a rabbit, mole, et al. Also, to add to the theatricality of the production, the actors can transform themselves from character to character in full view of the audience. In *The Fisherman and His Soul,* for example, to become the mermaid, an actress might simply wrap a pullover around her calves while the fisherman's boat is being set up.

PRODUCTION NOTES

(continued)

3. The risers should be sturdy but light enough to be easily assembled and reassembled into sets by the performers. The settings formed by the risers should be as simple as possible and just suggest the properties. A throne is a long rectangular riser as a back placed behind a short square riser which is the seat. This, along with one riser for a bed, is all that is needed for the throne room in *The Young King*. For instance, a boat is two long rectangular risers tip to tip for the prow and one riser for the stern. The plays move quickly and fluidly and the actors won't have time for more elaborate sets and they are not really necessary, since the narration and dialogue set whatever scene the audience needs.

J. T.

OTHER TITLES AVAILABLE FROM BAKER'S PLAYS

CANDIDA

George Bernard Shaw
Adapted and Abridged by Aurand Harris

Comedy / 3m, 2f / Interior

Probably Shaw's most popular play, *Candida* recounts the love sickness of young poet Eugene Marchbanks for Candida, wife of the Rev. Morell. At first, Morell is amused; but when he begins to doubt his wife's love, he becomes disturbed and angered. The poet becomes the stronger suitor, Morell realizes his weaknesses and Candida, one of the most remarkable women in dramatic literature, gives strength to her husband and teaches Marchbanks how to love. Harris offers a superb adaptation for competition, for study, and for introduction to one of the classics of modern theatre.

BAKERSPLAYS.COM

OTHER TITLES AVAILABLE FROM BAKER'S PLAYS

TARTUFFE

Adapted from Moliere by Charles Jeffries
and Luis Muñoz

Comedy / 8m, 7f

So virtuous is Tartuffe that every form of pleasure is an abomination to him. Orgon, a rich merchant, is completely duped by the ruse and watches approvingly as the cunning Tartuffe "reforms" his whole family. So besotted is the merchant that he even plans to give Tartuffe his fortune, his house, and finally his daughter! Orgon's wife finally exposes Tartuffe for the rogue he is – and her husband for being a gullible fool. By the time Orgon sees the light, only the courts can insure justice. This clever adaptation of the Moliere classic calls for an energetic ensemble. Moliere's greatest work is expertly adapted for one-act competition by the authors of *The Beggar's Opera, The Merry Wives of Winsor,* and *Valpone.*

BAKERSPLAYS.COM

www.ingramcontent.com/pod-product-compliance
Lightning Source LLC
Chambersburg PA
CBHW070241140726
47909CB00018B/1457